THE ASSASSIN IN 5F

NANA MALONE

COPYRIGHT

This is a work of fiction. Names, characters, places, and incidents either are the product of the author's imagination or are used fictitiously, and any resemblance to actual persons living or dead, business establishments, events, or locales, is entirely coincidental.

The Assassin in 5F

COPYRIGHT © 2021 by Nana Malone

All rights reserved. No part of this book may be used or reproduced in any manner whatsoever without written permission of the author except in the case of brief quotations embodied in critical articles or reviews.

Cover Art by Najla Qambar

Photographer: Brandon Sosa

Cover Model: Nana Malone

Edited by Angie Ramey

Published in the United States of America

1

LYRA

I had shot him.

My hands were slick with sweat, and I trembled as I sat in the darkness and waited.

I'd done it. Followed orders.

Center mass, point-blank, I had shot Marcus Black or whoever the hell he really was.

The man that I thought I'd been falling in love with wasn't real. He was a phantom. Just like the last man I'd thought I was falling in love with.

You know what they say: if you meet assholes all day, you're the asshole.

I'd fucked up. Again. God, what the hell was wrong with me?

You clearly have a type.

I must. Or, given what had happened, I was just a moron. Jesus.

Deep down inside, a small voice spoke up. *Maybe he was wearing Kevlar.* At The Firm, we had this specially calibrated, ultrathin Kevlar that we wore on missions. It could stop a bullet. It would hurt, but it *could* stop a bullet.

Which was why I was sitting in the dark on Marcus's couch in his apartment with my gun in my hand. Because he was coming back. He wasn't dead. If I'd shot him the way I'd been trained, he'd be down. But I hadn't. I'd left him an opening. But surely, he must know *not* to come back. Hell, if he'd shot me, there was no way I would be going home.

Unless you wanted payback.

And that was part of the reason I was there. I was worried. He knew where I lived, knew my routine. He could turn up at my job and take us all out with sniper fire from a roof somewhere.

I had to make sure he was dead.

Don't lie. That's not why you're here.

I didn't want to think about that. The real reason.

My stomach roiled and folded in on itself over and over again as I worried and waited. If he was interested in retribution, he could blow my cover. He knew all the ways to hurt me. He obviously was not the man I'd thought he was.

And you aren't the damsel in distress he thought you were.

I knew if I was smart I'd file an exposure report and be moved. He'd never find me. But instead, there I was, waiting in his apartment for him to return from the dead.

You really can pick them, can't you?

I didn't even know what I was doing. There'd be hell to pay when Roz found out he wasn't dead, and I'd had plenty of time to tell her my suspicions during the debriefing. Sure, we'd gotten the girl home. Made sure she was safe. Everything we're supposed to do. In that two-hour span of returning to headquarters, debriefing, and returning our weapons, I hadn't said a word.

Not once had I been like, *Hey, remember that guy you suggested I date? Turns out he is an Exodus agent and I shot him. Unfortunately, I'm worried that he is still alive, but I'm also worried he's* not *alive because I actually care about him like a dumbass.*

Fuck.

I ran a hand over my face, trying to calm the adrenaline. As high as it was spiking now, I knew that when it crashed, I would pass out and be vulnerable. And that wasn't something I could allow.

All you can do is wait.

My phone rang, and I answered it quickly, keeping my voice low. "Yeah."

"Are you okay?"

I breathed a relieved sigh. "Hey, Addie. Yeah, I'm fine."

"Are you sure? Listen, I wanted to talk to you. Can you get on a secure line?"

My secure line was in my apartment. "Um, not yet. There's something I have to take care of."

"Oh, enough said. You had to get some? Anything to ease that adrenaline, huh?"

I swallowed hard and lied through my teeth. "Yeah, you know me. Can I call you back?"

"You know what? Forget about it. Let's talk tomorrow morning, yeah?"

"Yeah. You're okay, right, Addie?" She was usually so together that I didn't have to worry about her, but she seemed off.

"Yeah, I'm just worried about the influx of Exodus agents. Something is going on."

"I agree. There's something we're not seeing."

"Let's talk about it later, but we need to figure that out."

Before we hung up, I asked the one question I'd missed during the debriefing. "How did we get the girl by the way?"

I could almost hear the smile in her voice. "I tased the fuck out of one of those Exodus agents. You should have seen him. He flopped around like a sausage."

"Jesus, Addie."

She just laughed. "What? It was a shame, too. He was built just like I like them. Tall, muscular, probably great in the sack. But Exodus, so yeah, can't hit that. I can't bone the enemy."

I coughed a laugh, trying to hide my misery. "Absolutely not."

Her words were soft. "Are you okay? You sound off."

"Oh, you know, just waiting for Marcus."

"All right. I'll see you later, okay?"

"Night, Addie."

I hung up my phone and leaned my head back. I was in deep shit. If I couldn't even tell Addie what the hell was going on, I was truly, completely alone.

MARCUS

Two nights after getting shot by Lyra, I watched her sit in my flat.

She shot me. That little bitch.

I couldn't believe it. After everything we'd done together, Lyra fucking shot me.

Did you think she wouldn't?

The only thing I could do about it was to bring her in.

Stop lying. You're not bringing her in.

I shoved down that bite of truth. I wasn't the only one on the team who had taken a hit. Someone had tased the fuck out of Rhodes. Procedure was to call it in, which I'd done. But I'd broken protocol when I hadn't divulged that I *knew* my shooter. She'd shot me with my own gun, which was humiliating enough in all honesty. But Rhodes had been tased. Why the fuck were they using Tasers? The agent who tased him could have easily shot him and taken him out permanently if she'd had a gun.

Something was not right, and I was going to find out why.

I'd been watching Lyra. She was smart. She'd gone to my flat. As far as I could tell, she was staying indefinitely. I'd been watching the cameras I had planted in the smoke detector and the television.

I thought maybe she'd give up when I didn't turn up the first night, but the next evening, as soon as work was over, she'd gone home to her own apartment, showered, changed, grabbed her weapon, and went back to mine. I knew that, because while she'd been at work, I'd planted cameras in *her* apartment too.

Why was she waiting after she'd shot me?

Maybe she knows that you're alive.

God, she'd shot me point-blank, center mass. If that didn't scream that the woman had no intention of me living, then I'd be damned.

She knows you're an Exodus agent, so she assumed that you were wearing protective gear.

My brain wanted to believe that she'd taken steps to protect me, but why shoot me in the first place? Yeah sure, she had orders to follow, but she didn't need to *shoot* me.

So what are you going to do about it?

I didn't know the answer to that yet. How long would she wait for me?

Rhodes had wanted to know why I was staying in the secondary safe house across the street, and I had told him that I felt like I was being watched. It was the only explanation I could give. I had been cleared right away for duty, but the doc had me riding a desk until I could breathe without stress again. All thanks to fucking Lyra.

I didn't want my place swept. I didn't want anyone but me finding Lyra there. So I told Rhodes it was clean. I couldn't tell him the real reason because then the team would swarm around her. There would be questions about how she knew who I was.

I had those questions as well. I had important things to ask her. Like, *was any of this real?*

For forty-five minutes, I watched as she checked the fridge, looked for a television show, and then watched out the window. But she wasn't scared.

Too bad little girl, you should be scared.

As she hummed to herself, I eased out of the shadows, carefully. Aware of the reflection on my windows.

Ten feet.

I watched her. Her curls bounced as she hummed to herself. I remembered the feel of them. The smell of her shampoo, the way she would have to twist her hair at night.

Her hair hadn't been curly two nights ago. She'd worn it straight. Did she straighten her hair for missions?

And then it hit me. The woman on the beach at Stellan Tusk's party. There was a reason I'd been drawn to her. It had been Lyra.

The Firm was all over this.

Five feet. Four feet. Three—

Before I knew what was happening, Lyra jumped up from the chair, turned around, and delivered me a thrusting sidekick that grazed my side as I was already deflecting it.

"Ah, glad to see you're still in fine form," I groaned.

Her eyes went wide as they roamed over my body. "You're fucking alive?"

"No thanks to you. I have to say, love, I'm really disappointed. First, that you shot me, which was utter bollocks, by the way. But then you somehow managed to not kill me."

She strategically moved closer to the kitchen, putting space between us.

"If I wanted you dead, you'd be dead. You seem to forget that we're trained for a bullet to the head."

I swallowed hard. She *was* trained for a bullet to the head, as was I. So why hadn't she done that?

"You and I are going to have a conversation about the people you work for and just how long you have been following me."

Her brows lifted. "*Me*, following *you*? Oh, that is such bullshit, and you know it. You're the one who targeted me."

I frowned. Something pricked at the back of my brain, but I ignored it. Now was not the time to get sentimental or start looking for a reason to believe her.

I pulled my weapon out of my back holster.

She smiled. "Oh, are you going to shoot me now? No silencer? Geez, you're really living on the wild side. One sound of that gunshot, and people would come running. And I don't think you'll be moving too fast. How's the chest?"

My voice came out as a growl. "Thanks to you, now I can't go on field duty for a minute."

"I could say I was sorry, but I'm not. You're a liar."

We circled each other. "Oh, really? That's ironic coming from you."

"You lied to me."

"We both lied to each other, sweetheart. And guess what? When we finally dropped the pretense, we actually connected."

She rolled her eyes. "As if."

"So you're telling me you didn't see me differently after we fought Prochenko?"

She sniffed. "So you do know who he is."

I grinned at her. "Of course, I do. Exodus has been after Victus for years."

"Don't you mean *working* with them?"

My brow furrowed. "What the fuck are you on about?"

She shook her head. "Everyone knows Exodus agents started working with the terrorists they once fought shortly after they split from The Firm."

I coughed out a laugh then. "Oh, really? Everyone knows that? What pack of lies are they feeding you over there, love?"

And then she did the unexpected; she lunged her whole body at me. I had to stumble to catch her, because she was right, I wasn't exactly in fighting shape at the moment. My shoulder hurt like a son of a bitch. I spun her around, ducked her punch, grabbed her arm, and turned her around to face the wall.

She heaved in front of me, her body quaking. And then her foot came down on my instep. I shifted my stance and held her hands over her head. I braced her in position with my hips while I patted her down for weapons. "No, you don't, you naughty thing."

I was too busy thinking about the way she was grinding her hips against mine, and I was so distracted I missed her sweeping leg. We tumbled to the ground with her on top of me. Despite the pain in my chest, I ground out. "Are we still pretending you wanted me dead?"

With ease, I rolled us over and settled my hips between hers.

She struggled in my grip, and I loosened my hold so that I wouldn't hurt her, but I didn't let her up. She narrowed her gaze then bucked her hips, one side higher than the other, rolling us back so that she was on top again. "I meant it when I shot you." Her voice was whisper soft.

"Liar." I lay beneath her for a moment, challenging her with my gaze. "Say you wanted me dead. Lie to me again while I can feel just how much you want me."

"I hate you," she whispered.

"I know."

She writhed against me like a wild cat, all fury and vengeance.

I tried to buck her, but she gripped and held on tight with her thighs.

I tried not to think of the last time she'd been on top of me just like this. The last time her hips had bucked on pleasurable terms.

The two of us rolled around the floor like that, each vying for the upper hand. I didn't want to hurt her. I outweighed her by fifty pounds, easy.

"Fuck, Lyra. Stop it. You're going to hurt—"

And then she delivered an elbow right between my neck and shoulder, and I yowled. "Goddamn it."

She scrambled away, trying to get to her feet.

I caught her foot and pulled her down under me. "Goddamn it, you *will* listen to me."

When I held both of her hands at the wrists in one of mine and placed my other one on her throat, she glowered up at me. "Fuck. You."

"We've already been there, remember?"

That caused more bucking. But without the use of her hands, it was harder for her to work herself free.

"Listen to me. Something is going on. You could have shot me properly two nights ago, using your training, but you didn't. And you were there at Stellan Tusk's party. You were the one on the beach."

She wiggled under me. She opened her mouth, presumably to tell me to go fuck myself again, but then her gaze flickered to mine. "I hate you," she repeated.

"No, you don't. For what it's worth, I don't hate you either. I shouldn't trust you, but I don't hate you. All you have to do is listen to me, Lyra."

And then the unthinkable happened. The more she wiggled and bucked, the more my cock thickened.

Her eyes went wide, and then her fucking pupils dilated.

I leaned down to growl at her. "Turning me on isn't going to end this conversation. We are going to talk."

"Oh yeah, you feel really eager to *talk*."

She lifted her hips again, and this time I groaned as her sweet heat came in contact with my rigid cock. "Little girl, if you keep playing with fire, it's not going to end well."

"Fuck you."

I dropped my head then and sealed my lips to hers as I groaned into her mouth. All the pain and anger from that night poured out of the both of us, throwing a large part of it over our bodies and lighting us both on fire.

2

LYRA

What was I doing?

My libido piped up immediately. *What you're doing is getting what you want.*

My hips were splayed wide open beneath Marcus as my tongue slid over his. He tasted of coffee and seriously bad decisions. And he still contained my wrists in his one hand. He was on top, and he was definitely in charge.

I wanted to break the kiss, to pull away. I wanted to stop, to make it end, but I couldn't. Every time I started to draw away, he would lick into my mouth just so and make this deep growling sound in the back of his throat. And I would be sucked in again.

Oh yeah. Marcus Black was definitely in charge.

And look, judge me all you want, but the moment he started moving his hips, I couldn't help but match his strokes. The zing of electricity that pounded through my body like a live wire was just too good. So damn good. And before I knew it, I was moving my body just how I needed, and suddenly, I had use of my hands. I should have been using them to hit him, push him off, get away. But instead, I slid my fingers into his hair and tugged. Bringing him closer, practically crowding me and shutting out all the light so that all I could see was him. He had taken over my world both physically and mentally.

It was him who finally dragged his lips away from mine. "Lyra. I need you."

This was where I should have shaken my head and told him to stop, where I should have said this is a bad idea. I don't want this. I don't love you. You're a liar and I hate you.

Instead, all I did was whimper and tighten my hold on the strands of his hair, pulling him down to me.

Because I was a glutton for punishment. Even though I knew the truth was that he hadn't wanted me, that I was a mark, I still wanted him badly enough to make this choice that was terrible for me. I was basically hooked on him. I had been jonesing and buzzing and needing him since that moment when we met on opposite sides, me with a gun in my hand. I'd wanted him then. I'd shot him, hoping that he would survive. Which told me I didn't know what was good for me because I was a moron.

And because I loved him.

Marcus rocked his hips over mine, hitting that spot just right, and I arched my back, trying to get closer, moaning as he nipped at my jaw.

"Fuck, you smell good."

"Hurry."

"Yeah. Next time we'll go slow."

Even his choice words of 'next time we'll go slow' should have set off alarm bells in my head. But in the heat of the moment, all I could think was, *Now, dear God, please now, make me feel good. Make me feel like I am on top of the world. Make me feel amazing.* Because I wanted this. I needed more. And only Marcus Black could get me there.

Stop overthinking and just enjoy this.

It was impossible to shut my brain off. I didn't know how.

But somehow, with Marcus's hands all over me, sliding, gripping, caressing, pinching... It got much easier.

When his hand slid up my rib cage and his thumb slipped over my nipple, my breath caught, and I bit out a curse. "Marcus. I need—"

His voice was more a rumbling vibration against my skin than actual words. "I know what you need."

That was all we said before we were tugging at each other's clothes. I could hear the tearing of fabric and feel the hard planks of wood beneath my shoulder blades promising me bruises later. But I didn't care. Because holy fuck, Marcus was alive, and my brain only cared about how quickly I could get him inside me.

Later there would be different words. Worried words, shameful words, but I didn't care right now because what was happening was louder, stronger, a cacophony in my brain. Marcus was licking at my skin with a sure tongue, teasing along the edges and the underside of my breasts. And I couldn't think. I couldn't even drag my eyes open because all I wanted was to let the sensations wrap around me and make me forget that he was the enemy, that I had been forced to do my job and shoot him. I wanted to forget that I could have lost this feeling. And suddenly, the relief of him being alive, the pain of the betrayal, and the driving need for him all hit a fever pitch, and I didn't know what to grab next. One second, I was tearing at his shirt, and the next, my hands were at his hair, tugging him down to me, desperate to have his lips back on mine.

Finally, I gave up on the shirt and just went straight for his belt.

I didn't even try and get the rest of his clothes off. I just unbuckled, unzipped, and slid my hand down into his pants to find him commando with a thick fullness jutting out to meet me. He hissed and then dropped his forehead to mine as he dragged in harsh breaths. "Fuck. Fuck, Lyra. Fuck me."

"I'm working on it."

Even his chuckle was a harsh gasp for air.

I stroked the silken hard length of him from tip to root, and when I reached that spot just on the underside of his crown and stroked my thumb over it, his entire body shuddered over mine. "Jesus Christ, Lyra. Do that again and I'm going to come."

I teased him once more. "You're not coming."

"You are a naughty thing. You know that, love?"

The pang of that word, *love*. I knew it was just a Briticism, a piece of slang. I knew it wasn't true but still, hearing him say it made something inside me twist. Had we been different people in different circumstances, that word could have meant something. But it didn't. Right now all that mattered was us together. What we could get from each other right now.

Pleasure.

He reached for my hand, and I loosened my grip. "Fuck, if you keep doing that, I can't think."

I opened my mouth to argue with him that I didn't need him to be thinking. But then his mouth was on mine, and I could hear the tear of more clothing. Next thing I knew my shirt was torn open and he was working on my leggings. He tugged them part way before his hand crept down my belly, under my panties, and he slid two fingers inside of me.

I threw my head back and arched my back. "Oh my God. Oh God, yes."

"Did you miss me?"

I couldn't even find the words. All I could do was nod my head and grunt. "Uh-huh. Missed you."

"Yeah. I missed you too. You haven't been letting anyone else poke around down here, have you?"

His fingers drove deep, and I screamed, "No. Fuck no, it's you. It's only you."

"Yeah, that's what I thought."

And then he rewarded me, or punished me, however you wanted to look at it, with a stroke of his thumb over my clit.

I squirmed against the pressure. I wanted more. I wanted him to slow down. I wanted him to stop.

No, not stop. Keep going. But God, I wanted control. That's what I wanted. Control over the situation, control over what my body was feeling, a way to look at this from a fifth-story view. But Marcus was demanding so much more. He was demanding a ground-level view, a harsh look. Because he was driving me toward the outcome that I needed so badly. The one I thought was spiraling away from me. And then as suddenly as he'd started, he slowed and then stopped. I whimpered. "Hey."

He lifted his head up and kissed my nipple then grinned at me. "Oh, you didn't think I was going to let you get off that easily, did you?"

I wiggled my hips, and he laughed, bracketing one hand on my hip to keep me still. "Oh no. When you come, it's going to be around my cock. I just wanted you close to the edge quickly."

And then he pulled back, pressing a brief kiss to my hip bone before sliding down my body and pulling my leggings completely off, tossing them haphazardly across the room.

He only managed to get his cargos partway off his hips before his cock jutted out. I stared down at it. Proud and thick and long, knowing exactly how he'd fill me up. Exactly how there'd be that slice of burn upon entry. How I'd have to accommodate his size.

How he'd take his time and then speed it up. How I'd beg, whimper, ask for anything.

I knew how this went.

He settled between my legs, gripping his big hand around the base of his cock and lining himself up to me. He teased my slickness and rubbed the tip of his cock against my clit, making me shake. "Fuck. I'm so mad at you, but I can't not have you." The words tore out of him.

I raised my hips, trying to get him exactly where I wanted him.

And then he stilled. "Fuck. Condom."

He reached for his wallet in his cargos, quickly sheathed himself, and then with no preamble, he notched himself against me and drove home.

The litany of curses that fell off his lips would have made me blush if I hadn't been too busy teetering on the edge of orgasm and screaming, "Oh my God. Oh my God. Oh my God."

He seemed to agree as he whispered, "So fucking good. Jesus. I'm done for. Absolutely done for." And then he dropped his lips to mine in the most tender kiss we'd shared since I shot him. It was more a mingling of breaths with a light dusting of our mouths. And when he started to move, he cradled my head. Then, bracing himself up on his elbows, one hand scooted under my back and cupped my ass, bringing it closer to him but also protecting me as much as he could from the hard floor. Neither of us suggested moving, though.

Oh no. We were screwing on the floor of his living room on the hardwood. So desperate to get more of each other, desperate to chase the high. And that's what it was, a high. As he rolled his hips and kissed me and growled, one hand tugging my hair, the other holding my ass, bringing it closer and closer with each thrust of his hips, his lips laid claim to mine. Banished any thought I had that I wasn't his or that we weren't real. With bruising and punishing kisses, long slides of his tongue into my mouth, the ownership was complete. No matter what happened from this point forward, I belonged to him. After all, he'd licked me, hadn't he?

This wasn't lovemaking. It wasn't even just sex. It was

possession. Because even though I'd shot him, he still wanted me, and I still wanted him. And that's just the way it was.

He set a punishing pace with me just grabbing onto his shoulders for dear life and trying to hold on. He didn't relent until I started to quiver inside. The angle he held me at helped too, because with every stroke forward he brushed my clit, and I shuddered. He tore his lips from mine. "Come on, Lyra. Just give me what I want. Just give it to me."

I didn't even know what I needed to give him until he kept rolling his hips and driving into me. Making it impossible for me not to— "Marcus. Oh Jesus."

The orgasm came from left field, a complete surprise as I was just trying to hang on for the ride. My brain was still too focused on all the things that weren't quite right. But that orgasm snuck up behind me, chased up my spine, and then bitch slapped me so hard I saw stars.

All the while, Marcus just drove forward. Making love to me, owning me. Loving me. "Yeah, that's it. Let go."

And let go was the only option I had.

Because all around me as the earth shattered, all doubt fell away, all worry fell away, all anger fell away. And I knew where I belonged.

Even as I screamed out his name, Marcus buried his face in my neck and inhaled deeply. "Fuck, yes. Yes, Lyra."

It wasn't until the aftershock began to take me and I started to come down off my high that I realized he'd stilled. He held himself completely stock-still as I rode out my orgasm. "Marcus?"

"Yeah, baby?"

Again, his voice was more of a rumble against my skin than anything. "But you didn't—"

"Oh, we're not done."

He picked me up easily, keeping himself inside me as he

rose and moved us to his couch. He sat with me on top of him and said, "Oh, this is perfect."

Still more aftershocks took my breath away as I settled over him and he hit so deep inside me. My eyes went wide, and all I could do was blink and watch him.

His smile was slow. "Now, love, why don't you show me all the ways you wanted to punish me."

I knew I should be mad. So mad. All the mads. But in this position, with him hitting so deep I could feel another orgasm riding, being mad was the last thing on my mind.

I notched my hip just so, and his eyes rolled in the back of his head as he muttered a curse and his hand slid up to cup my breasts. At one point I stopped and reversed the motion of my rolling hips, and his head snapped up. His eyes narrowed and became hyper-focused on me.

"You're evil, woman."

"Am I?"

We watched each other, our gazes locked, as I made him feel how he'd made me feel. Owned. Like there was no other alternative for him but to be mine forever, even if he was the enemy. I could feel him expand inside me, getting even harder. He was losing control.

When I leaned forward, he matched me, bringing his lips to my nipple and sucking gently, making me gasp. Oh God, that felt so good. But it wasn't what I wanted. I wanted to look at him as he came.

With my hands in his hair, I tugged his head back right before I stopped all motion and deliberately massaged the length of his dick with my internal muscles.

His eyes went wide, and his hands went to my hips, digging in. "Lyra."

I kept up the little massage, the tiny grips of his cock until suddenly he was moving his hips. And then we were moving together. Eyes locked in this game of who would give up control first.

And the good news was it was neither of us. Because the only way for either of us to have real power was for us to share it.

His lips fell open and I leaned forward to nip them. His hands dug into my hips, and I could feel him stiffen in my arms. I heard him whisper my name on his lips over and over and over as a reverent chant. "Lyra. Lyra, oh my God. Lyra. Lyra."

And as he fell over the edge of oblivion, I wanted to maintain my smugness, but I couldn't. Because I was falling right over with him.

I was done for. I was completely in love with Marcus Black, and he was the assassin in 5F.

MARCUS

I had no idea how long we sat there. The two of us, panting, trying to catch our breath. Every movement triggered an aftershock, and one of us would shudder and just grip on to the other.

This was the kind of sex you read about. The kind of sex your friends tell you about that you've never experienced before until you found someone who was a near fucking perfect match.

Jesus. Every time she moved, I could feel the tremors in her sex along the length of my cock, and I groaned. "Oh fuck, do you need to do that?"

"I'm not doing it on purpose."

She might not have been doing it on purpose, but my cock liked everything she was doing.

My bloody cock couldn't be controlled. And he twitched awake.

Oh fuck.

She stared at me. "Again? We've done that twice."

"Yeah, I know."

I pulled away from her, hissing at the sensitivity.

But the moment she was off, she darted for her clothes, and I went to the bathroom.

Once I was rid of the condom, I grabbed a spare change of clothes from my room.

I came back to find her dressed and holding her gun again. "Ah, back to that. Okay, well, where did we leave off? Oh yeah, you had just shot me, and I was on the ground. Begging for mercy."

"Why do you work for Exodus?"

I stared at her. "Me? Why do you work for The Firm?"

"You know I have to take you in."

"Oh yeah? How are you going to explain why I'm still alive?"

"Because they don't know that you were the Exodus agent I shot."

"Oh, and you expect me to quietly not tell them?"

"God, why is this happening?"

I softened my voice. "I don't know. But Lyra, I'm not the enemy."

"Right. So you keep telling me."

"Look, I know you don't believe me, but it's not what you think. I'm not working for terrorists. Look at who you're working for."

"You wouldn't dare tell me that the firm is a terrorist organization."

"No, I'm not going to tell you that. I'm going to tell you to look at it for yourself. The girl we were both there to rescue, she's a pawn. Logan Brodick wanted to leverage Max Teller.

I'll bet you anything that when you returned her home, Teller agreed to the merger for TBC Oil with Franklin Oil. And taking his daughter was a way to make him cooperate. Fall in line."

I shook my head. "I don't know anything about that."

"It was supposed to look like a simple kidnapping and rescue, but it's more complicated than that. I'm not lying. Have a look for yourself. You'll see I'm telling the truth. The Firm isn't as squeaky clean as they'd like you to believe."

"And I should just take your word for it?"

I shook my head. "No, of course not. That's not who you are, and I wouldn't respect you if you just took me at my word. Do some digging for yourself. You'll see I'm telling the truth."

"Fine, I'll do some digging, but I'm not saying you're right."

"Of course you're not." I chuckled low. "What I'm saying is, you're smart. You're going to go look and see if anything I say rings true. You know what to do with that. All I'm trying to do is get you to ask some questions."

"You don't know me as well as you think."

"Yeah, I do. Present activity notwithstanding, you're too smart to sit down and just take it. So figure it out. Figure out what's going on."

"So what, you're not just going to jump out and say you're alive?"

"No. Because right now The Firm doesn't care. They don't know me or that I was the one you shot. You didn't tell anyone the agent you shot might be alive. And I don't think you're going to tell them now that I am."

"That's an awful lot of trust."

"Yeah. But I know you. You're going to do the right thing. You always do."

"Like I said, you don't know me as well as you think you do."

"You know what's interesting, Lyra? I may not know you, but I also *feel* like I've known you forever. Have a look for yourself. If you don't find anything, don't believe me. But if you do find something, come find me, and we can talk about it."

She glared at me. "I'm not going to find anything."

"Yeah, if you say so."

And then I let myself out of my flat, still feeling the buzzy side effects of being inside her. I knew what had happened between us couldn't happen again, otherwise, I'd be endangering my whole team. The next time I saw her, it was going to be strictly business.

Liar.

3

LYRA

I lay awake in bed for hours afterward. I could still feel him all over me. And even though I'd showered in an attempt to wash off his scent to try and pretend that hour in his apartment had never happened, I could still feel him.

Marcus black was in my soul. And considering that I had shot him and he hadn't died, he was like some kind of avenging angel hell bent on revenge. And the revenge he planned for me involved several hours of torturing me with orgasms.

How could you do it?

I wish my subconscious was asking how I could have had sex with him knowing who he was. *What* he was. But really, the question, if I was being honest, was about how I could have shot him. The relief I had felt when I saw his face coming out of the shadows was palpable. I could taste it. Hold it between my fingers. It wasn't ephemeral. It had weight.

And it had meaning. Because it meant that despite trying to hold back, despite trying to distance myself and my heart, I cared about him. Marcus black was under my skin.

And even knowing how dangerous that was didn't seem to

engage my brain into stopping this from happening. Because it was already too late. I *wanted* to believe him. I wanted a world where I could still have what he'd given me on that floor. The heat, the desperation, the complete and total ownership.

And this wasn't some case of him owning me in some patriarchal kind of way, but more along the lines that we owned each other. I'd been just as desperate as he was. And that feeling, when he first sank deep as he bit my bottom lip, I would never feel that feeling again. Relief, rightness, soul-aching tenderness, and fury all rolled into one.

Fury because how dare he lie to me. How dare he make me believe he cared about me and then turn out to be someone I didn't know at all. And then how dare he insist that he cared about me and that his lies were a necessity.

You told the same lies.

And that's what was making it so hard for me to hang onto my fury. I had lied to him too. I had looked him in the eye and deceived him. That was the job. But for once I wondered, where did the job end and Lyra begin?

So now, I throbbed for him, ached for him in a way that I had no business feeling. Like his cock had left an echo inside me, staking its claim and making sure everyone knew that it had taken up residence and nobody else would ever be able to fill its place. And there was also that place in my heart that no matter how many times I tried to board it up, it still ached and pinched in want of its freedom. And wanted to be free to care about him, even though he was telling me things I couldn't believe. Even though I thought he was still lying to me.

He wasn't right. There was no way he could be right.

How could everything I'd been told about my life be a lie? And worse, how could he be so great? After all, we'd all been told what Exodus agents were like. We'd been told about their cruelty, their manipulation. That we had better shoot first and ask questions later if we encountered one of them.

But he dared to challenge everything I'd been taught. And I wanted to just believe that he was lying, but I couldn't. He could have killed me, but he didn't. He could have reported me, and he hadn't.

It's all part of the manipulation.

Or was it?

There was one way to find out. All I had to do was verify whether or not he'd been telling me the truth. I could walk into records and just look up the information. But I told myself I wasn't going to do that because he was obviously lying. That's what Exodus agents did. They were liars.

But so are you. Wouldn't you like to know the truth?

So I spent the night tossing and turning, thinking about Marcus, his hands, his mouth, his dick, and most importantly, his words. By the time I got ready for work, I wanted to exorcise him from my brain, and there was only one way to do that.

So now, like a fool, I was doing the one thing I'd told myself I wouldn't do last night.

I knew what I was doing was dangerous. It was a bad idea. It was all the things you're taught not to do in Espionage 101. Don't spy on your own team. And if you do spy on your own team, don't get caught. But there I was in the archives, looking through things I had no business looking through.

I didn't want to believe Marcus. I was determined to prove him wrong.

Are you sure about that?

I had security clearance for the records room. It was where new agents learned about past missions. Learned the players and the history. But some portions of the records were not entirely accessible, and that was where I was getting creative.

You know something's wrong.

I knew no such thing. I was only getting peace of mind. At least that was what I was telling myself, but something inside me believed him. Exodus was a problem that wasn't adding up.

I needed answers.

I pulled the files of our last mission.

Everything seemed fine on the surface, perfectly normal. Then I dug in and looked a little deeper. The girl's father, Max Teller, was the head of a multinational oil company. There was a big deal coming up related to a merger.

I quickly scanned over the information.

And then I saw that her father had been the only member on the board of directors who voted against the merger and acquisition.

The way their board was structured, they needed a unanimous vote. Everyone had to say yes.

And he had said no.

So someone kidnapped her? Who would do that?

The question was, who had the most to lose? I pulled up files on each of the board members. The ones with the most to lose and most to gain.

Are you sure this is a rabbit hole you want to go down?

I couldn't help it. I was already on this path, already digging in places I shouldn't be digging.

And then I found what I was looking for. Tucked away in one of the files, I found an outgoing encrypted communication dated two days prior to our rescue mission.

Had someone notified Exodus that we would be there?

As I continued to search though, no other communiqués were encrypted.

"So why this one?" I muttered to myself as I wondered if I could have it decrypted.

For that, I needed a hacker. Someone who could keep their mouth shut. For obvious reasons, I couldn't use anyone internal. But I had a couple of sources who might work. They were

Addie's people though, so I was going to have to reel her in if I wanted answers.

I quickly downloaded the file and checked over my shoulder. The key to doing something that you were certain was going to get you in all kinds of trouble was to look like you were supposed to be doing it.

Anyone who looked suspicious was immediately suspect. And the last thing I needed was another psych eval.

Another quick sweep had me further down the rabbit hole.

I could hear Marcus's voice in the back of my head. The girl's parents didn't contact The Firm. They'd tried to handle it privately. And there it was, tucked in another nondescript file like it was completely unimportant. Never to be examined, but it was right there in front of me.

The request for extraction, also encrypted. The question was, why? This was one of those things that was important for newly recruited agents to learn. Why we got involved, what situations warranted our involvement.

There was absolutely no reason to encrypt that communiqué.

The other anomaly was that the request hadn't initially gone up through the usual chain. This one started at Command then filtered down to us.

No, this hadn't come in as a normal request, which meant it was a favor. But for who?

Maybe that's why it was hitting me wrong. The way we normally handled requests was to examine protocols and other mission parameters. Determine what was urgent and what wasn't. A knock request was a personal favor, but for who?

The more I dug, the less I found. Dammit, who was important enough for a request like this? And if it wasn't the girl's parents, then who?

A sick feeling swirled in my gut. *Was Marcus right?*

Had he been telling the truth? All this time, as I'd been fighting him, had he known something I didn't know?

And if Marcus was right that the request didn't come in through the usual channels, then who the hell had we handed that girl off to?

I did a quick search, and soon discovered that mere hours after the board of the oil company unanimously voted for the merger, Max Teller received the happy news about a reunion with his daughter.

I sat back in the chair with the proof in front of me. "Holy shit. Marcus was right." But there was another problem. Someone had sent an encrypted communication out from The Firm just hours before our mission. But to whom, and why? That's what I needed to find out.

MARCUS

"Do you want to tell me what the hell you're doing here?"

"If I said no, mate, would you leave me be?"

Rhodes leaned over and glanced out the window. "And I ask again, why the safe house and not your perfectly good flat across the street?"

"It's not a flat, mate. You're slipping."

He frowned at me. "Sorry, it's these meds they gave me. I make more mistakes with them on board. I'll get it handled. Are you tight bro?"

I shrugged at his casual switch to American slang . "I feel fine. I get the odd metallic taste in my mouth, but the doc says my concussion symptoms should be clear in another day or so, and after that, I'll be cleared to be back out in the field."

He nodded. "Yeah, all right. Are you going to talk to me about it, or are we going to do the thing where we pretend everything is fine?"

I shrugged, wincing slightly. "Are we going to do what?"

"Talk about that fucking bruise you have on your chest. How did it happen?"

"I got shot," I said with a huff of laughter.

"Yeah, but bro, I know you. You would have fought like hell. So what actually happened? We didn't find a body."

"Yeah, you would have fought like hell too, but you got tased, didn't you?"

He scowled at that. "And you know what? I'm pretty sure it was a woman."

I frowned. "Why do you think it was a woman?"

"I don't know. She seemed to do it *gleefully*."

I laughed at that. "And you think the person who attacked me was a woman too because she was gleeful about it?"

"Yeah. It's like under the mask, she smiled, you know?"

I laughed so hard. "Mate, you don't think that's a stretch?"

He pressed his lips together. "No, I don't think that's a stretch. We both know The Firm uses whatever tricks they can. Watch, they've dug out someone from my past and hired her just to fuck with me."

"You recognize that that sounds paranoid, right? I thought you were the one over here trying to convince me that *I* was mad."

"Well, you're mad, of course. But that's nothing new."

Rolling my eyes, I asked, "This personal vendetta that the Firm has against you... What did you do?"

"See, this is where I can't tell you things."

I chuckled to myself. "Yeah, well." I wasn't exactly telling him things either.

I hadn't mentioned a damn thing about Lyra. And as it was, he was circling around far too close to the mark. "So, why are we hiding here instead of in your flat?"

"I'm not hiding."

Liar.

"Dude, if this isn't hiding, I don't know what is. And the fact that you're watching your current flat tells me a lot. Who do you think is following you?"

"I just want to keep an eye on things."

"Isn't it easier to spy on your girlfriend if you're actually, you know, *in* the building?"

"I'm not *spying* on her. I'm watching my place. I know Curtis, Maggie, and Michael think that there's nothing to be worried about, and I don't really think there is either, but I'm thinking better safe than sorry because... I don't know. Something's been off ever since Stannis Prochenko showed up. To keep her safe, I'm easing out of the equation."

He watched me shrewdly. "You think I don't know the smell of bullshit?"

I decided to come a little clean with him. "I got shot. But I have the impression the person didn't *want* to do it."

He frowned at me. "So you're telling me the person who shot you didn't *want* to shoot you?"

"If they'd shot me properly, I'd be dead. We both know that. From what we know of The Firm, they're really efficient."

He pondered that. "Yes, we were both lucky."

"That's just it. I don't think luck had anything to do with it. I've got theories percolating. I'm just working it out."

He nodded. "Right. What are you going to tell Lyra? You've gone to visit an ailing aunt in the UK?"

I scowled at him. "I don't know what I'm going to tell her yet."

When in fact, I'd already tried to tell her something. We'd gotten a little distracted, of course. A shiver ran through me at the memory. I wanted her so bad.

But it wasn't sustainable. One of us was going to slip up and expose the other. Either that or one of us was going to end up dead. I really, really hoped it wasn't the latter.

Rhodes just watched me and waited.

"Rhodes, what would you think if I asked you if you thought we'd been sold a bill of goods about The Firm?"

He laughed. "What's that supposed to mean?"

"We know The Firm supposedly works with terrorists, right?"

"Everyone knows that. They put on a front, but they have ties to sources of the biggest terrorist agencies in the world."

"Yeah, but what if they've been told the same about us?"

He laughed. "What's with all the what-if scenarios? Obviously, they can tell themselves whatever they want in order to survive, right? We know the truth."

"Yeah, but how do we *know* it's the truth?"

He frowned then. "What the hell are you saying?"

"I don't know. We say it's the truth because it's what we've been told. But what if the truth is somewhere in the middle?"

"Are you suggesting that they're not the devil? They're responsible for a lot of hell. They traded that kid to a power broker. Her parents got her back, but only after her father agreed to a merger his board of directors was pressuring him to approve."

"I'm just saying, could it be we haven't been told the whole story?"

He stared at me like I was losing it. "Mate, of course, we know it was The Firm. That's straight from intel."

"Yeah, but intel can lie. There is something else going on here."

"You have really been thinking about this."

"Mate, all I'm saying is, things don't add up... We're playing a game of life and death. We need to be certain."

He clapped a hand on my shoulder. "There's nothing more certain than us being the good guys. Recognize that."

"I'm not arguing that point. I'm just wondering if the agents at The Firm are dirty after all."

4

LYRA

I was just coming out of a mission debrief when someone grabbed me from one of the darkened side halls.

Instinct kicked in immediately. I twisted at the hold, managed an uppercut, which was blocked, and then someone wrapped their arms around me tight. Hot breath tickled my ear. "Hold fucking still. I'm not going to hurt you."

A shudder rolled through me as recognition hit. "Fuck you, Tyler."

He released me gently, easing me away from his body. "Look, I didn't mean to frighten you, but I wanted to talk to you for a minute."

Talk my ass. Surprising an agent like that could get someone dead.

"About what? You and I have nothing to say to each other." I struggled in his grip. I was still secured around my neck, but he wasn't trying to hurt me.

"Lyra, can't you see I'm trying to help you?"

"How is that exactly?"

"Whatever it is you're doing, whatever it is you think you're chasing, you need to stop."

"Fuck you, Tyler."

"Been there, done that. You know what's really funny? It won't be the last time either."

"You wish. Now let me go."

He sighed. "One of these days, your little tantrums, your little *I'm Roz's protegee and nothing can touch me* thing is going to get you killed. You need to be more careful when you're nosing around where you don't belong."

"Is that a threat?"

"It's a warning. Can't you see I'm trying to help you? Tell me what you were looking for."

"You know, even though you're saying the right words, I don't think you actually know what help means."

He sighed. "I know you went on a little adventure today and had a look through the records. I know you downloaded data."

I swallowed hard, working to keep my face neutral. How the fuck did he know? Was he the one who had the alert set up? "I don't know what you're talking about."

He grinned. "Ah, you're a better liar than you used to be. But lucky for you, I have a level-five clearance. I went back in and erased your tracks. You're welcome."

All I could do was blink, stupefied by what he'd said. "I didn't ask for your help. Moreover, I haven't done anything wrong."

He swallowed hard, his gaze locked on mine, his lips a hair's breadth away. If he wanted to, he could kiss me.

Inwardly, I shuddered, resolved to bite his tongue if he did. But the adrenaline dump of real fear made my body loosen. "Tyler, why did you come back? You were assigned to London. I was perfectly happy when you were there. What is the fucking purpose of your return to LA?"

"Roz reassigned me."

"Yeah, I know that, but it doesn't explain why you said yes. You're level five. You get a say in your assignments."

"Maybe I wanted to see you again."

I scowled at him.

He winced. "You're still mad? Way to hold a grudge."

"I'm supposed to forget when someone used me, embarrassed me, humiliated me in front of my colleagues? Yeah, that's easily forgettable."

He sighed. "It's not how I wanted it, Lyra."

"I don't care. Are we done here?"

"Not until you tell me what you're looking for."

"None of your business." There was a part of me that wondered if maybe I could trust him, but then I remembered everything he'd done and wondered what was wrong with me mentally that I'd even considered trusting someone like him. "I have nothing to say to you."

He ran a hand through his hair. "You are always so fucking stubborn. Just listen to me for a minute. I am on your side. I'm trying to look out for you."

"Do you think I'm dumb enough to believe you? Let me go."

Kramer, another level-five operative, rolled by us and gave Tyler a smirk.

I growled at him. "I fucking hate that that's how they all look at you. Like you're the man or some kind of player and I'm the sad sack who fell for it."

His gaze shifted back to me. "That's not how anyone sees you. When are you going to realize that everyone really respects you?"

"Yeah, if you say so."

He sighed and released me. "Whatever it is you're doing, you need to be more discreet."

"Go to hell."

"I am not your enemy, Lyra."

"Aren't you?"

The muscle in his jaw ticked, and then he sighed. "You're asking the wrong fucking questions." He reached for me again, tucking a finger under my chin. "When you finally realize at some point that we're on the same side, I hope it won't be too late."

I wrenched my chin away. "Don't touch me."

"Right. It won't happen again. It's that guy, isn't it?"

"What guy?"

"The one who came over here, throwing off all the *she's mine now, asshole* vibes. He at least looks like the type to protect you."

"When will guys like you realize that girls like me don't need protection?"

"You don't need *physical* protection. You're the strongest operative I've ever known. But you need to watch your heart. Someone is going to trample on it, and it's going to be ugly."

"Newsflash, asshole, *someone* already has."

He nodded and stepped back. "Yeah, I'm that asshole. So at least let me fix what I broke. If you want some information, ask for it. Don't go digging in places that are public where someone can see you. Find someone you trust and have them do it. Never get it yourself. You were almost caught today. Be more careful."

I searched his gaze for some kind of explanation. "Why are you helping me?"

He sighed. "One day, you're going to figure it out." Then he turned his back and stalked away.

When he was gone, I sagged against the wall, trying to catch my breath. And that was how Addie found me.

One look at my face and she said, "What the hell just happened?"

LYRA

I dragged Addie to the coffee shop off the corner of the park near the office and spilled my guts, and all she did was stare.

Full stupor. Slow blinking. Several attempts to open her mouth then close it and stare.

Addie blinked at me once, twice, a third time. "You shot Marcus?"

"Yes, but only because he's Exodus." I really needed her to catch up.

"Then he rose from the dead, and you had dirty sex on his apartment floor like a couple of wild animals."

I wrinkled my nose. "Well, to be fair, he's not *undead*. This isn't one of your paranormal romances, but yes, there was sex..." I shifted in my seat at the café, watching the light play off of my glass.

She smirked. "Dirty-talking, pull-your-hair sex?"

I rolled my eyes and shrugged. "Yes. Damn. Would you focus?"

She sipped her tea. "Okay, I just had to let that sink in. You had that kind of sex we dream about and you didn't call me. It's fine."

If fine meant slightly irritated. "I'm sorry, okay?"

"Apology accepted," she said hastily. "Now... What the fuck? He's Exodus?"

That was the appropriate response. "I know. How did I not see this?"

She seemed to ponder this a moment. "Okay. And well, to be fair, he didn't know you were Firm. You are both excellent liars."

"What am I going to do?"

"Right now, nothing. We need to dig further into his claim."

I pulled out the flash drive with the files I'd downloaded from records. "Already on it."

"Fuck, Lyra. Is this why Tyler cornered you? Did he catch you in the act?"

"No, but he claims to know what I did." I sighed. "I had to know."

"Does your faith in Marcus have anything to do with the orgasms he gave you?"

Maybe.

"No, it has nothing to do with fucking orgasms. He didn't need to come back. He didn't need to try and convince me that he was one of the good guys. He could have just run. Acted like nothing happened. Instead, he came looking for me. Which told me that he was telling the truth. Or at least some version of it."

She shook her head. "But the night of the mission, you said he was down."

"Well, he *was* down. Now he's not."

"You know how to kill, Ly." With a deep breath, she added, "So what are we going to tell Roz?"

That was the problem. If I told her I'd disobeyed a direct order, I'd be done. "Nothing, because what I saw on record tells me that at least some of what Marcus says is true."

"And that leaves us with us possibly having a mole. You need to get in front of this. Cut Tyler off at the pass. He clearly is up to no good."

"But with what? She'll need proof."

She pointed at my flash drive. "Buy yourself the time you need to get it. Report him for his stunt in the hallway."

"You think that will work?"

"You were seen, right?"

I nodded. "Yeah."

"Then it's enough to plant doubt," Addie said. "And in the meantime, we find out who sent this communication."

"That's the plan." I just had no idea how.

"And don't think we're done with the Exodus agent either. We just have bigger fish to fry." Addie winked at me. "Just try not to shag him again until we know if he's evil, okay?"

My mouth fell open. "It's not happening again. Ever."

"I love you, Lyra, but given the way you're shifting in your chair, the question is when and not if."

Damn her to hell. She was probably right.

5

LYRA

"Are you sure you want to do this?"

I stood behind Addie where she sat in the desk chair in Marcus's apartment. We were going to hack into the fucking Firm like a couple of crazy people. And I certainly didn't want to do it at home. It was unlikely that Marcus was coming back.

Is that what you want?

"Yes, I want to do this," I said with false conviction.

"All right, I'm going to ping us off several relays, but we need to get information and get out. We can't fuck around. We need to be stealthy and fast. Do you understand me? No dicking around because you think you see something interesting. Do you get me?"

"Yes, yes. Hit it and quit it, etc., etc."

She shook her head. "We've been friends too long."

"Yes, I know. But you want answers too. Better we do it together."

"Yeah."

Her fingers flew at the keyboard. I was wondering why she never became a tech, but then I remembered one time she told me she preferred the action. She didn't want to be just stuck in the office. Which I understood. That need to be able to feel like you were making a bigger difference, I got that.

I watched her while biting my nail anxiously. And then she clapped her hands. "Hot damn, that worked. Start the timer."

We knew we didn't have long. And after Tyler's little stunt, I knew he was watching us, or me anyway, so we really had to do this fast.

"Um, records. Files. Send relays. Check any other mission where Exodus showed up."

She nodded and kept typing. "Okay, I see the send relays. Looks like it was two messages."

My belly knotted. How bad was this?

Addie's hands stopped moving. "Holy fuck."

"What is it?"

"The communication lists locations, dates, and agents on the mission along with skill sets."

"No." My world axis spun. I hadn't believed Marcus, but he'd been right. Did that mean someone had told Prochenko where to find me?

"I know what you're thinking," Addie said.

"How can I not think it?"

She tapped on the keyboard, and I could only presume she was logging out.

I said, "Look, it doesn't make sense. I want to point the finger at Tyler, I do. And I think he's definitely up to something, but he didn't show up until *after* Prochenko."

"Yeah, but you know what? Prochenko really did go after you, specifically. He stole your purse, remember?"

I ground my teeth, thinking of that purse. My fucking purse. My *mother's* purse. Asshole.

"Okay, so it was just pure luck that I had Marcus with me?"

She shrugged. "Maybe. I wish I could say more."

We kept looking and I checked the clock. Sweat started to drip between my shoulder blades. What we were doing was an enormous risk. Tyler had already warned me that he'd erased my impromptu walkabout in the records, so I couldn't help feeling uneasy. Why had Tyler helped me? Was he somehow involved in any of this?

"Can you do me a favor? Just take a look at Tyler's files."

She blew out a breath. "Oh, thank God. I didn't think you'd ask."

"I want to know what he's up to and why he helped me."

"Yeah, I wondered about that too, but let's just both agree that he's not to be trusted."

"Of course not."

"I know you have a soft spot for him." She slid me a side-eye. "I'm just making sure that you're not falling for that again."

"Um, I already have one guy who I know I can't trust. I don't need to do it with another."

SHE POINTED AT THE SCREEN. "Here, on the Damascus job. Tyler was part of the mission, and the target was rescued. But when I looked at the follow up, it seems the victim's husband stepped down as finance minister right before his wife was rescued. Just like our last job."

LYRA

This was a risk.

But maybe Roz would be willing to listen. All I had to do was convince her I was scared of Tyler and didn't just have some petty vendetta against him. Which, for the record, I did not.

Liar.

When I knocked on her door, she glanced up from her paperwork. "Hi, Lyra. What's up?"

"Do you have a minute?"

She nodded. "For you, always. Shut the door." I went in, wiping the sweat off of my hands. She didn't miss a beat. "What's wrong, honey?"

"I need to talk to you."

She laughed. "Let me guess, Tyler?"

I took a deep breath to steady myself. "Yes. I have some concerns."

"You know what's funny? Earlier, he was in here talking to me about you."

My stomach muscles turned to Jello. "What?"

"He said that you're making impulsive decisions in the field."

Who the fuck did he think he was? Did he really think he was going to get to me through my mentor?

"I'm following my training."

She steepled her fingers. "I hate to agree with him, but we both know you *do* tend to be impulsive."

She might have been right, but the sting of betrayal pierced me. "Right."

"Oh come on, Lyra. *You* know you're impulsive. *I* know you're impulsive. Hell, it was one of the reasons I selected you. You think fast on your feet. When something goes wrong in the field, you rely on your training, but you rely on your instincts too. I would say you're probably too emotional, but your impulsivity? That's why you're here."

"Poor impulse control. Tyler makes me sound like a serial killer when he's the one with a screw loose."

Her lips pulled into a wry smile. "Oh, hush now. What's the problem?"

"Look, I'm not a child coming to complain about her little brother." Sort of.

"Oh, good, because that would be awkward, considering the two of you used to, *you know*."

I rolled my eyes. "This isn't funny, Roz."

She put her hands up. "Okay, sorry, it's not funny. But you have to see the irony in the two of you coming to me to mediate."

"I'm not coming to you to mediate. I'm worried that Tyler is up to something. Yesterday he cornered me and threatened me. I even have a witness."

Her eyes went wide. "That's a serious allegation."

"Don't believe me? Ask Kramer. He saw us."

"He saw *what* exactly?"

"Tyler attempting to choke me out." Okay, it was a mild exaggeration. I could have fought off any real attack. But still.

She sighed and sat back. "I see we have a problem."

"You think?"

Then she asked me the unexpected. "How are you feeling after the shooting?"

I kept my face perfectly neutral. "I feel fine."

"On comms, you seemed *hesitant*."

"Well, everyone's been all up my ass about not killing anybody *anymore*."

She nodded. "Not up your ass, Lyra. I just need you to preserve human life."

"Except not Exodus human life?"

"Well, we're to preserve human life that could be useful. How's that?"

It bothered me what a loose relationship we had with who was useful and who was not. That would never sit well.

Roz continued. "I hear you where Tyler is concerned. There are other factors in play here, but I'll speak with him."

I stared at her. She'd *speak* with him? I'd told her I had

proof of him choking me, and she was going to speak with him. "Excuse me?" My brows rose.

"Let's just say I'm aware of your history together. I know the two of you don't always make the best decisions when it comes to each other."

"Wow."

"Just speaking the truth, love. You both make the worst decisions when the other one is involved. So I already had someone watching him. And you. But you've been surprising. I thought you'd be mooning after he returned to LA, but it seems that you have actually gotten over the events of last year around your breakup."

"I have a job to do."

"And I have to tell you, I'm impressed that you listened, because I know how difficult that is for you."

"Difficult? Is that what you'd call this situation?" My heart hammered against my ribs.

"Look, let me talk to him. I'm going to look into it. I am listening to you. I know you don't trust him. And if there's a fly in my ointment, I want to know. In the meantime, Lyra, you know it's been a while since you've had a vacation. I think maybe you could use a few days off."

"I don't need days off."

"Lyra, I told you already. You work too much. You work too hard."

"And I told you, I like working. It means I don't have to sit around doing nothing. I hate that."

"It also means you don't have to think. You don't have to be alone. A few days off will do you good. Take a week."

I ground my teeth. "Roz, I'm telling you, I don't need—"

"We all need some time to reset, Lyra. I promise you. In the meantime, I will look into this. But please be careful. We all know how dangerous Tyler can be. He might have a pretty face, but he can be treacherous. And I want you to be cautious."

It was the first time she had acknowledged that Tyler could be dangerous to me. But again, like that was information I didn't have. She'd just never said it out loud before.

"Okay, I'll take a week. But can you please keep me posted on what's happening with this?"

"Yeah, I'm on it. And Lyra, thank you. What would I do without you as my right hand?"

"Luckily, you don't have to find out."

I walked out, hoping to God I'd done the right thing.

6

MARCUS

Touching Lyra had been a mistake.

You think?

I sat across from Michael in our central conference room, needing some answers. The walls were dark and stoic, the lights harsh.

Michael asked, "How are you feeling? Rhodes mentioned that you are now taking up residence at the safe house."

"I am. Just making sure. Nothing like getting shot center mass to shake things up for you."

Michael rubbed his jaw. "Right. So your shooter, was she Firm?"

He was trying to trip me up. "I didn't say my shooter was a female."

Michael just grinned. "Listen, Marcus, we're just trying to do the right thing. Help us help you. It can be heard on the comms playback from that night."

"Actually, you know what? I know one thing that can help me. I want to know about The Firm. You were here in the early days. What happened?"

Michael sighed. "It's old news."

"It's not old news to me. And if it can still affect me, then I want to know. The agent, the one who shot me, seemed to be under the impression that I was an Exodus agent hell-bent on murder."

Michael frowned then. "That's bullshit."

"Yeah, I know. But that's what she believed. It's why I was unceremoniously shot, so I need someone to explain it to me."

He sighed. "All right, fine. When Orion McClintock and Aiden Saint-James formed The Section, they had a joint philosophy. Right the world's most evil and deadliest wrongs. For ten years, they managed to overlook their differences. And then they couldn't, so they went their separate ways. And in that transition, there were some who prospered."

"Terrorists?"

He nodded. "Yeah. Among others. Lots of bad guys with political agendas, and a few who are more interested in sowing the seeds of chaos and lining their own pockets but not in doing any real damage."

I sat in steady silence as he spoke, hoping anything he said might help fill in the blanks.

"Yeah. In the early years after the split," he continued, "it was chaos. And as we started to work with different governmental departments, there was competition between the two organizations. But you know the folks with letter agencies. They don't really care who they use as long as they have *someone* to use."

"Okay, so when did The Firm go bad?"

He ran a hand through his hair as he sat back. "Rumor was, that's why they broke up in the first place. Because Aiden Saint-James was in bed with terrorists."

I frowned at that. "Was it proven?"

Michael shook his head. "On several missions, agents were lost and important files went missing. During the reorganization of the two agencies, terrorists prospered without anyone to keep them in line. It was a shame because McClintock and Saint-James were as tight as brothers."

"So no one tried to verify The Firm's ties to terrorists?"

"Are you kidding me? Of course, I tried to verify. There were two agents known by their call signs as Rogue and Renegade. They tried to leave the Firm. They had information on all their dirty dealings. They were married, I think, but they were killed."

I shook my head. "Fuck."

"Yeah. They were supposed to meet with one of our top Exodus agents and expose everything. But then, poof. They never showed and were never heard from again. The Firm must have found out what they were planning."

"Okay, but you've never been able to get another agent to turn?"

He shook his head. "No. By now, they have things locked up tight."

I watched him. I'd played poker with him before and knew the man really had no tells, but there was something about his eyes that told me he was holding back, so I took a chance. "Or you have an agent undercover there already."

He lifted a brow. "What makes you say that?"

"You have someone in place, but they don't have enough clearance, right?"

He sat back then. "You're grasping. I don't have anything to tell you."

"Of course, you don't. Just level with me. What are we dealing with? These people, they killed Simone."

He sighed. "*Someone* killed Simone. All common sense currently indicates that it could have been Firm agents, but we don't have proof of that."

I gave him a frustrated sigh. "I hate that bullshit. You and I both know what happened."

"Yeah, we have an idea. But we like proof, not ideas."

"Right. Proof."

"Sorry, but that's the way we roll."

"All right fine, who's your agent on the inside?"

He shook his head. "You know full well I can't tell you that."

"Tell me something, anything."

"Just know that we've got someone who is gathering actual evidence. When they plan a mission, we sometimes get a heads-up. Then we have to make decisions about what we're willing to interfere with."

"And if we don't interfere, people die."

He sighed. "And there's nothing we can do about that."

"Fucking hell. You know that's bullshit."

"I know. So why don't you tell me about the Firm agent who shot you?"

I stilled, marveling at his ability to flip the conversation so easily. "The agent could have killed me but didn't. They broke protocol."

He nodded. "But why?"

"I have no idea." The lie was bitter on my tongue, but I needed more assurances before I could divulge anything about Lyra.

He smirked then. "One of these days, you'll stop playing things so close to the vest and recognize that I'm actually here to help you."

I laughed. "Sure you are, mate."

"You don't trust anyone."

"No. Not since Simone, I don't."

He sighed. "Is there anything I can do to change that?"

I shook my head. "No, but this was helpful. Has your mole brought in anything new?"

He shook his head. "No, I haven't gotten anything since the last mission went sideways."

"And where did you find this mole?"

"Let's just say they were burned by The Firm. They have a vested interest in seeing the scales evened."

"So I won't show my intel, and you won't show yours?"

Michael shrugged and then grinned at me. "You know how this works."

"Right. Well, I'll give it some thought."

"Yeah, you do that. In the meantime, stay safe. Did the doc clear you for duty yet?"

I shook my head. "No. The quack has benched me for another week."

He grinned then. "Maybe keeping you off the grid for a moment isn't the worst thing in the world."

I grumbled at that. "Right."

"If you're going to do something stupid, do me a favor and tell me first, okay?"

"Sure. Will do."

He shook his head. "Something tells me you most certainly will not."

7

LYRA

"Goddamn, why does that feel so good"?
"I hate you."
"You only wish you did."

That exchange while Marcus was inside me made me shiver. And even in my sleep, I could feel every nip and bite and lick. His hot breath along my cheek and the way his fingers circled my clit as he drove inside me. The way he kept me hovered just at orgasm, teasing me, all the while giving me exactly what I needed. It was like all the masks were off at last, and we could finally see each other for what we really were. And it was so good. Beyond good. That kind of sex that people tell you about when they're on vacation, it was exactly that. And fucking hell, I needed it. I needed it so bad.

And just as my body was going to take me back to that moment where I tipped over into blissful oblivion, I heard a noise.

My eyes immediately popped open. A sense of alertness came over my body like a splash of cold water, complete with floating icicles that landed squarely on my libido. I was awake and ready to rumble, but not in a good way.

I reached under my pillow, my fingers clasping around the butt of my gun. Who the fuck was inside my apartment?

I took two deep breaths. *Steady on, Lyra, steady.*

Maybe I'd misheard. Maybe I was imagining it. Maybe…

No fucking maybes. Now was not the time for maybes. There was most definitely someone inside my apartment, and I had a feeling I knew who it was. Also, I was going to kill him.

You only think you're going to kill him. Since you were dreaming about him, you're more likely to fuck him first.

I expected a wash of shame as my own body and brain reminded me just how badly I wanted Marcus. But no, no shame. Just a tacit acceptance of *hell yes, I want the man*, though I knew I couldn't trust him. But that didn't mean I didn't want him.

Bloody fantastic. Silently, I slid the sheets off of me. My feet landed on the rug at the side of my bed, giving me two feet of silence before they made any quiet friction sounds on the hardwood floor. I'd gone to bed in my Beyonce racerback tank. It was thin and threadbare and offered not an iota of support for my C-cups. I eased over to the side of the bed where I kept my extra mag and tucked it into the back of my panties.

There was a part of me that thought, *Hey, fighting with your tits flapping in the wind is probably not a great idea.* At the same time, was I going to really risk opening a drawer to grab a shirt?

Beyonce, emblazoned on my tank, and her middle fingers, which were now very conveniently placed at my nipples, was just going to have to cover me the best she could.

The sliding door that normally closed off my bedroom was ajar enough for me to ease through, deliberately and on purpose. A quick peek at the reflection in the mirror on the side panel of the door showed me two shadows. He'd come with a friend. Naughty, naughty Marcus.

The problem was, without the aid of light, I had to fight on instinct. Because once I stepped foot into the room, I would have no help. The shadows were not going to be enough to provide cover, but they also weren't light enough to show me my opponents.

Stepping into the room, I breathed deeply. Once. Twice. And then I caught a movement, more felt than seen. It was the mildest shift, but I knew what it was.

I turned on the heels of my feet, aimed an elbow, and caught the assailant right in the kidney.

All I heard was grunting pain. I already had his arm behind his back and had him pressed up against the wall, but that left me vulnerable to the second intruder. I jacked his arm hard, heard the crunch and him yelling in pain. And with his widened stance, I also delivered a swift knee to his balls. I knew I had at least a few seconds to completely incapacitate him while I had the upper hand. I was certain I had broken his arm.

But then there was a whizzing pop right by my fucking ear.

It was so close, I felt the heat singe my hair just a little.

Before I went to bed, I'd pulled my curls on top of my head, hoping to maintain them and not have to re-twist my hair until the next night. I was grateful for it, because that bullet certainly would have whizzed right through, burning off a good chunk of it.

I left the groaning one and ducked behind an art sculpture I'd picked up in Nepal, annoyed that it might get destroyed in this melee. And then I tucked and rolled, turning and aiming the gun toward the shadow, squeezing off two rounds.

I heard a curse, and then someone dove behind the couch.

I was moving quickly in the dark, aided by the knowledge of exactly how my apartment was laid out.

As I bolted over the coffee table and ducked onto the couch, I aimed my gun and shot through the upholstery, wincing at the thought of replacing it.

But then a shadow I hadn't seen, two of them in fact, came out of the second bedroom. I only managed to get one shot off before whoever was behind the couch reached up and grabbed me by the neck.

His lift was swift. Suddenly, my airway was closed as I was slammed down.

The hard jolt of my back cracking against the coffee table made me wince. But I knew I had to conserve energy. Relax my body.

But he was squeezing my throat, so I reached up, creating space between us. Just enough to wedge my shoulder up and grab him by the balls, squeezing hard and then tugging.

He cursed, loosening his hand just a little, enough for me to draw in a deep breath. With air in my lungs, I lifted my head and butted it against his forehead, hard. That forced him to let go. And with his legs open on top of me, I delivered another knee, all the while rolling him off as we tumbled off the coffee table together. I was swinging, delivering quick, lightning-fast jabs.

Behind me, there was a fight. Wait... Two of them were fighting each other?

What the fuck was going on here? How many people were in my apartment?

My gun had fallen between the couch and the coffee table, and I dove for it.

Just as my hand gripped it, the guy I'd been fighting grabbed my leg, and I faceplanted on the couch. But I had my gun now. I reached around my side, fired off two rounds, and then all I heard was a thud as he hit the hardwood.

I had ten feet to the door, but the two men, I assumed they were men because of their sizes, were fighting too close to it. One or both of them might stop me.

Why were they fighting?

The only option was the balcony.

In just my panties and tank top, that was the last way I wanted to go, but I didn't have a choice. I bolted, hitting the button for the blinds, trying to duck under them as I shoved the door open.

But when the blinds went up, in came the light. And when I turned to make sure they weren't chasing me, I saw one of the men was Marcus.

He was fighting the others. The original man whose arm I'd broken was flapping around, reaching for his gun, aiming at Marcus. I turned my gun, pointed at him, and fired a headshot.

I aimed for Marcus and the man who was fighting him, but they were grappling too close together and I couldn't risk taking a shot.

What are you doing? Run.

I knew the protocols. Run. Call in. Request backup. Except, fuck. I couldn't leave Marcus.

I went back inside where it wasn't safe. Back toward the man I wasn't even sure I liked.

Oh, you like him all right. Or at least part of him.

As they fought, with the added aid of light, I could finally see. I didn't know the other men. Who had I fucking pissed off this time?

As Marcus took a hit to the face, I barreled into the man he was fighting and jumped on his back, locking my arms around his neck and squeezing. He tried to shake me off, but I hung on tight with both arms locked around his neck, choking out his airway and trying to keep in position.

He backed me against the wall and kept bashing.

Marcus was up. He appeared to be momentarily stunned as we fought. But when his brain came back online seconds later, he raised his gun, fired, and the man I was fighting fell face-first with me on top of him.

"You fucking took your time there, didn't you?"

"You're welcome, by the way."

I blinked up at him. "*I'm* welcome?" My hair had fallen out of the pineapple. It was cascading around my shoulders in wild curls. "I had to come back and save you, dumbass."

"And you could have taken a Victus hit squad by yourself? Is that what you're telling me?"

"What the fuck are you even doing here?"

"I was watching your place. You know, keeping you safe."

"Newsflash, asshole, I'm a spy. I don't need protecting."

"Well, this assassin," he said, using air quotes, "just saved the spy's life. How's that?"

"You're still mad I called you an assassin, aren't you?"

"Yeah, a little bit."

I surveyed the chaos that laid before me in my apartment. "What the fuck just happened?"

"Clearly, you can't stay here anymore."

And then he stopped talking. I wasn't sure why until I realized how cold it was and I glanced down to see my tank had shifted and both my breasts were pointing straight at Marcus.

MARCUS

It happened so fast, I don't think either one of us were prepared for it. One moment, my eyes were glued to her breasts and unwilling to move. But my training took over when, from her bedroom, a shadow formed.

We were both so busy bickering and thinking about her tits that we almost missed it. Even as he raised his gun, I was already turning to pop off a round. But he was faster.

All I could do was whip back around to try and catch Lyra, take her to the ground, protect her, shield her.

But I was too late. I was too damn late. Next to me, she crumpled, holding her side and squirming.

Fury flooded my veins, and I turned and emptied my clip

into the fucker that had come out of the bedroom. *One. Two. Three. Four.*

That's all. Those were all the bullets I had left.

When I was certain he was down, I kneeled by her side. "You're going to be fine, Lyra. You're going to be okay."

She wheezed and coughed, and I ran to the bathroom to get supplies. When I had collected towels and gauze and antiseptic, I leaned over her. "Okay, we're going to get you cleaned up."

She shook her head. "No. Oh my God, that hurts."

"You're fine." She had to be fine. I *needed* her to be fine. Because what if she wasn't?

This cannot be like Simone again.

I tried to shove out the thought as I worked on her. Towels for pressure. And then I worked rapidly to suture. "It's not going to be pretty."

"Fuck you, I'm pretty regardless."

I laughed at her ability to still cuss me out while I was busy trying to stop her from bleeding out. "The shot was a through and through, but we've got to stop the bleeding. And I'm going to need to get you somewhere safe."

"My apartment was safe."

"Oh yeah, so safe."

More glowering. As if it was my fault that she had Victus all over her place. "Would you just hold fucking still?"

"Well, maybe if you weren't trying to hurt me."

"Oh, honey, when I want to hurt you, you'll know."

She hissed several curse words at me. Honestly, how was this my fault?

But still, I worked quickly.

Don't look at the blood. Don't look at it.

As I worked, the memories of what had happened with Simone started to filter through. I had to blink rapidly to clear my eyes.

"I'm the one who was shot," she said, "but you look like shit. Are you okay?"

"Yup. Fine."

"You know, you don't look fine." She hissed a breath as I patted an antiseptic pad. "Let *me* do this. You don't get to play doctor right now."

"Well, considering you're the one currently responsible for scarring *my* bikini body, I'm going to play doctor."

"If you wanted to play doctor with me, all you had to do was ask."

I liked it better when she was like this, feisty, fighting.

The wound really was a through and through, but she was bleeding a lot, so I was worried about internal injuries. I could only staunch the bleeding and do a thorough check later when I knew we were safe. I had to get her out of the apartment.

I guess it's a lucky thing you were watching her like a pervert.

I ground my teeth. That was the last thing I needed to think about because, yes, I had been watching her place like a pervert.

"How did you get here so fast anyway?" she asked curiously.

"Is this the part where you're going to be grateful?"

"No, I'm not grateful. You haven't answered any of my questions."

"You focus on getting better. Let me work."

"Well, in case you hadn't noticed, you're pressing on a bullet wound, so maybe you could talk to me and distract me from the pain?"

"I am not interested in distracting you."

"I knew it," she said. "You're a sadist."

"Hardly."

"I repeat, how did you know they would come for me?"

I sighed. "It was easy. Victus has been casing your place for over a week."

"What do you mean over a week? I didn't see anything?"

"That's because you weren't looking for the right things."

She rolled her eyes. "Oh, right. And you were?"

"Who's responsible for surveillance at your apartment?"

Her brow furrowed then. "The Firm handles it."

I looked her in the eye. "Then someone at The Firm is very, very bad at their job."

"You're saying someone was willing to let me die?"

"Yes. If this was *my* team, the whole place would be swarming with Exodus agents by now. But your so-called team hasn't sent anyone in. Someone is letting your arse flap in the wind. Not a good move."

She swallowed hard. "I don't believe you."

"Lyra, these are just facts. You had six Victus agents in here. Six. All sent to kill you. You think that this was a random burglary?"

"How do I know this isn't Exodus?"

I gestured to myself and my uniform and then gestured to the man down on the floor. "We wear black camo. They wore all solid black. Simple. Unidentifiable. We don't even look the same, Lyra. And regardless of who was here, the point stands that you have no backup from your team."

She furrowed her brow at me and coughed. "My people wouldn't leave me like this."

"One of *your people* is willing to let you die."

"No. I need to call it in."

"And you will, from somewhere safe."

"And let me guess, you've got somewhere safe?"

"Yes, I do, as a matter of fact. We'll pop by my place for more supplies."

"What, so you're going to take me to Exodus? Am I your prisoner now?"

"If you want to play a prisoner game, we can have fun with that. But no. I just want to keep you off the street and intact for now. We'll come up with a better plan when we have some breathing room."

She winced as she pressed her side that I'd just applied the gauze to.

I had hidden the medical tapes with the gauze and eased it down. "It's rough and dirty, but it'll do the trick. It'll hold."

"Thank you."

I blinked down at her. "What? Was that an actual word of thanks?"

"You know, I liked you a lot better before. You were less of a dick."

I chuckled then. "I like you a lot better now. You're mouthier. I can see the real you peeking through."

"Was that a barb? Because let's be real, we were both lying."

I pressed my lips together. She had a point. We had both been lying to one another. And I could be mad at her for it or accept it.

She raised one brow. "You recognize I didn't tell you who I really was because it was classified, right?"

"Same. So we're in the same boat. We lied to each other, and we have no idea of the truth about each other. So we can fight about it, or we can get the hell out of here."

8

LYRA

"What the hell did you do to her?"

Addie sounded annoyed, and I wasn't sure exactly what was wrong. Everything was fine, right?

I was floating down, and I tried to turn into it and find solid ground, but a searing pain sliced through my side. Then I sat up with a jolt. "Fuck me."

Addie was quick to my side. "Oh God, she's still bleeding."

Then there were hands. So many fucking hands on me.

And then I remembered. Marcus. Marcus was there, and I'd been shot.

Bit by bit, the events of the last few hours came back to me, including my demands that Marcus use my phone to call Addie and let her know what happened.

Marcus's voice was like whiskey promises. "Hold on, love. We're checking your suture."

That seemed perfectly reasonable. Once I was fully awake, I knew not to move. I felt the pain. "I'm fine. I'm fine, Addie."

"Sorry to break it to you kid, but you hardly look fine."

"It's just a flesh wound. It hurts like a son of a bitch, like someone stabbed me with a hot poker, but other than that, I'm fine." Funny thing was, I didn't sound fine.

I lifted my head and watched as she checked Marcus's work. "All right. I guess in an emergency, this isn't that bad. Let's get a fresh dressing on it, and then we'll get her cleaned up. Did you give her antibiotics?"

Marcus shook his head. "Not yet, but I have some here, fortunately. I'll have someone drop a fresh pack off at the new safe house."

Safe house? Was that where we were? I didn't remember much after stopping at his flat for supplies. By the time we stepped outside, my vision was graying.

I remembered nothing after that.

A quick glance around told me I was in a minimalist apartment. Cold gray walls. Barely any furniture. No personal touches. *A blank slate*.

"You thought of everything. Too bad you're a big dick."

I heard Marcus mutter something under his breath along the lines of, "Well, I *have* a really big dick."

When Addie turned to me, she smirked. "He's hot, but he's rude."

All I could do was laugh. "Would you two stop bickering for a moment, please? My head hurts."

Marcus disappeared for a second and came back with the antibiotics and a glass of water that I downed.

Once Addie had my wound cleaned and rebandaged, she sat back and asked, "Who came for you?"

I shook my head. "I wish I knew. I was dead asleep. Next thing I knew, I had guys in my house who were very enthusiastic about putting holes in my body."

She turned and scowled at Marcus. "And just how did you end up there?"

"I'd been watching her place," he said matter-of-factly.

Her brows lifted.

He only shrugged. "It's a long story."

Addie stepped back. "Oh, it's my night off, so I have time. Explain this long story to me."

I cleared my throat and filled her in on the details.

"After our research session yesterday, I went home to bed. I didn't talk to anyone." Addie frowned. "And there was no way anyone could have trailed us. We were clean. So what the hell?"

"Unless someone has had a plan to attack Lyra while she's vulnerable all along. Victus has been watching her place for a week."

Addie shook her head. "Impossible. The Firm does regular sweeps."

"Like I told Lyra, someone hasn't been doing their job."

Addie sat on the edge of my bed. "There's no way. I'll talk to Roz. This has to be a mistake."

I shook my head. I knew what she was feeling. The same slice of betrayal that I'd already experienced. "Until I know what's going on, we tell nobody."

"You don't mean Roz, though. She trained you."

I hated it too. But a hit squad had come to my house. "Not even Roz, Addie. I mean it."

"Jesus, this is messed up."

It was only going to get worse. "Ads, we've been fed a bill of goods about Exodus. I don't think they're any worse than we are. The point is, someone's gone out of their way to make us believe that they are."

"You're saying someone at The Firm wants us to not trust Exodus?"

"I'm not sure. But we need to look into why. The truth. I'm tired of being dicked around."

Addie ran her hands through her blond curls. "Okay, so do you think someone inside The Firm told them where to find you?"

"Yes."

"But to send six guys after you? That's overkill. You send one assassin. A sniper on a roof somewhere takes you out with a single bullet. Reasonable, if you can call it that. Not in your apartment while you're sleeping. Even then, you send just the one. Not six."

My stomach knotted, twisting and turning in a ball that bounced all over my belly. "Someone wanted to make sure, I was very, very dead. The question is, why?"

Addie frowned. "Is it Tyler?"

"I'm not sure. It could be."

Marcus frowned. "The same twat I met at your office that day?"

I pursed my lips at him. "Yeah, that's him."

"Your ex?"

I sighed, seeing where this was headed. "Yes, my ex. But honestly, I'm not sure you can even call it that. I was only an assignment to him."

Marcus's brows lifted then. "An assignment?"

"Yes. When I started as an agent, I was too green. If there were any sexual situations on missions, I essentially froze up. I couldn't do my job. So Roz had Tyler brought in to teach me how to be more at ease. He's very good at his job, because he managed to convince me we actually had a relationship beyond him teaching me to be at ease with my body."

"I hate that arsehole."

"Yeah well, that makes two of us."

Marcus turned to Addie. "I have the proof her place was surveilled."

Her gaze snapped to his. "Show me. Maybe I'll recognize someone."

Addie crossed her arms as she studied Marcus's laptop where his surveillance of me for the last week had been recorded. "I'm telling you, Lyra, Tyler is fishy. His appearance back in LA was timed with Prochenko's reappearance and all these missions where we've had exposure. And okay, fine, I'm willing to accept that maybe Exodus isn't as bad as we've been led to believe, but those missions have all nearly gone bad. And this isn't the first time. Three years ago Tyler was on several missions that went wrong. I always assumed that's why he got transferred to New York for a while."

"My brow furrowed. "You think they sent him for retraining?"

"Your guess is as good as mine. I always thought retraining meant that you would never be seeing them again, but he's still kicking."

I frowned. "I'm not sure how we keep chasing Tyler down. I have been ordered on mandatory vacation by Roz. I don't want to expose you, Addie. I do want to know what Tyler is up to, though."

"I'm going to keep looking into him. He's going to make mistakes somewhere. What are you two going to do?"

Marcus rubbed his jaw. "Let's go back to the beginning. Prochenko came after us. So it's back to him. Let's figure out what the fuck Victus wants with us."

LYRA

"Can we trust her?" Marcus asked.

In the dark, in our new safe house, I lay wide awake, wondering how this was now my life. What I should have been doing was going into the office to confront Tyler. But something was off there. My mentor was either protecting him or couldn't see what I saw. So going to Roz wasn't safe. And currently, I was meant to be on vacation.

If I used the next few days carefully, I could come up with incontrovertible proof and be rid of him. I just had to stay this course that I never planned to be on. This was such bullshit because I loved a plan. I thought about plans, executed them, made backup plans for my plans, and this whole depending-on-other-people thing was really sticking in my craw. And now this fool was asking if I could trust the only dependable person in my life?

" Yes, we can trust Addie. Besides, she's all I've got at the moment. Roz has to follow protocols."

To my left, his voice was low. "I'm sure I don't have to tell you what will happen to us if the wrong people get hold of your location right now."

I resented that nudge. As if I didn't know I'd almost died. "What is your problem with her? With us?"

"I don't have a goddamn problem. This isn't personal. When are you going to see that?"

"You know, it *feels* personal."

He sighed. "I get that. I really do. But I'm just trying to keep you safe."

"Why? Obviously, what we had wasn't real." Even as I said the words, I didn't believe them.

He was silent for a long moment. "You know, I could spend the next three days trying to convince you that it was real, but you've already made up your mind."

"What am I supposed to think?"

"You're not supposed to think anything. I just want to keep you alive."

"So I'm just another job to you?"

"Christ, you are so unbelievably stubborn. I can't even imagine what it's like to be that stubborn. You can't see the truth when it's right in front of you. To me, what we had, that shit was real. And I'll be damned if I let another woman who I love die when I could have done something to stop it." He dragged in a deep breath. "So think what you want. I'll just be over here saving your arse."

What was that? Did he just say—

My brain couldn't even process the words that had come out of his mouth. "Wh-what did you just say?"

He sighed. "You caught that, did you?"

"Well, you threw it out there, how could I not? Why would you say that?"

"Because it's true."

I swallowed hard. My insides melted at the words and the idea that he could care about me like that. I just wasn't sure if I could believe him. I'd been lied to before.

"Look, you don't have to say it back. You don't have to get in your head about it. Just know that I'm going to keep you alive no matter what it takes. We're going to find out who's after you. And then when all is said and done, we'll both go back to our lives."

"*Can* we go back? It's not that simple."

"Well, like I said, the idea is that if we figure out who the hell is after you, we clear it up, make sure you're alive and okay, and then you and I can go back to our separate corners. We don't have to do this anymore."

I wasn't sure why, but that hurt. Even though I knew he wasn't who he claimed to be. Even though I knew that this couldn't possibly be real.

But he said he loved you.

He wouldn't be the first. And he probably wouldn't be the last. In this line of work, who were we if not our deceits, our lies, the little things that we had to tell ourselves to get out of bed every day? Like, I'm not a murderer. I'm not an assassin. What I do is for the greater good.

Except *was* it?

"I don't even know what to say, Marcus."

"It's fine. Just think of me as someone who's here to help you resolve whatever this is, and then it'll be over and you won't have to see me anymore."

Because I didn't want to touch what he'd said, I scooted around it. "Are you talking about your fiancée?"

When he spoke again in the darkness from the floor, his voice went soft. "Yes. Her name was Simone. She was an agent too. There was a raid in one of our safe houses where I was recuperating after I had been severely injured. She, uh, she didn't make it."

I could hear myself say the words as the pain and sadness struck me. "Jesus, I'm really sorry."

"It was a hard lesson to learn. But yeah—I won't let you be a sitting duck." There was a beat of silence. I couldn't even let myself process his words, so I shoved them down to join the other feelings I didn't let myself deal with. "Thank you for telling me about her. She must have been something if she was another agent."

"Look, I don't want to dwell on that, okay? We'll hunt down this weapon Victus is after. They'll be forced to talk to us then. Once that's done, you never have to see me again. I will get reassigned, and then you can move on. Matter of fact, you can even move on with *Tyler* if you want."

I rolled my eyes. "That's a low blow."

He chuckled. "I mean, really? That guy?"

"He was different then, just so you know. Really sweet."

"Right. Really *sweet*."

"Hey, he was nice to me. I felt important. Seen."

"I find it hard to believe that you were that naive. The guy is a dick."

"Clearly, I have a type," I muttered.

I heard a slapping motion as if he'd clutched his hand to his chest. "Ooh, that was the low blow. But really... I'm sorry he hurt you. He was a fool."

Somehow those simple words settled in deeper than anything else I'd told myself over the years. Which was bullshit because I didn't need him to validate me or my feelings.

But it felt nice knowing that someone else could see what Tyler hadn't. God, I was pathetic. Even I knew it. Tyler was a fool. A moron. A grade-A asshole. "Yeah, thanks."

"It's just the truth. Don't get all wrapped up in your feelings about it."

I rolled my eyes. "God, were you always such an annoying asshole?"

"Yes, but you were distracted by my body."

"Stop it."

He chuckled. "Well, I'm just stating facts, love. It's up to you to believe them or not."

"I thought you were stating facts before, too. We probably have to have all of our date conversations over again now. Wait, do you even have a brother?"

He laughed. "Yes, I do."

"Well, okay. At least that wasn't a lie."

"But I have a niece, not a nephew."

I grumbled. "Of course, you do. You know, it's funny because even though I was lying to you too, it just... I don't know. It feels worse, being lied to."

"Yeah." He was quiet again for a moment. "Why do you think the dating app matched us, anyway?"

In some ways, that was a tough question. Because there was a part of me that was convinced that the dating app was broken. Flawed. But I could see myself with him even when we'd been fighting. We'd been a hundred percent in sync.

"It probably saw something compatible about us when we answered the questions honestly. Except, we couldn't exactly be honest with each other in person."

"And isn't that a shame? We would have probably been having a lot more fun."

"Probably."

"Where did you go when you disappeared on that first date?" His voice was low, mellow.

I laughed at his question. "I had a mission in Bulgaria. I was chasing a human trafficker."

"Ah, I've been rethinking a lot of that. All those little things you would say and do. I'm supposed to be great at catching liars, watching people. But I ignored every single clue from you."

I laughed. "Well, I ignored your clues too. Where did *you* go on our second date?"

He laughed then. "God, my excuse was the worst. I mean, come on, food poisoning? But I couldn't think of anything better at the time. I had to fly to Chechnya. After a bomb maker."

"Christ, that was you?"

He chuckled. "Yup."

"Wow, your team did good work there. We wanted to go after that bomber, but Roz told us we'd lost the lead."

If he was surprised by my magnanimous attitude, he didn't say anything. But then his next question threw me. "Why did you try to break things off after the third date?"

I thought hard on that one. "I was trying to keep you safe. I was worried Stannis was after me."

"God, you pretended to let me teach you how to fight," he laughed. "Who were you fighting at the Bacchanal?"

"Victus member, since Stannis was a no show."

"Of course, you were able to stay on mission."

"If I recall, you were trying to distract me. You were on a mission too?"

"Only one of us was doing great at our job that night. Christ, you fight like a demon. I can't believe you convinced me you needed training."

I laughed. "I will say you were a very good teacher."

"How were you ever able to hold back in that fight with Stannis?"

I laughed. "Well, remember all those drunken boxing

movies back in the day? I just pretended I was doing one of those things. Execute a strike, act like I was falling over."

"You let me sit there like a twat showing you how to make a fist."

I could hear the consternation in his voice. "Yes, but you wanted to do it. You were so sweet."

"Yeah, just what every man wants to hear, how *sweet* he is."

"Well, you were."

"I was trying to keep you safe from muggers. How was I supposed to know you were an assassin?"

"You know, I've been asking myself that same question. Neither one of us saw it. To me, you were cute and geeky."

"Ah, so you thought I was *cute*?"

"Really? Out of all these admissions, that is what you're focusing on?"

"Yup. My ego knows no bounds."

I laughed at that.

He could still make me laugh. He could easily wear down the barriers of my distrust. "Why were you suddenly so intent on us continuing to see each other?"

He laughed then. "Well, after the fight, it was like I was seeing you for the first time. Once I saw you fight Stannis, even doing your *I can't fight* act, it was like I couldn't get you out of my head. You were so full of strength and tenacity, and honestly, it was all I could think about. Your unwillingness to give up. So yeah, total turn on. Also, well, by then I knew what you tasted like, and I was certainly unwilling to give that up until I'd had more."

My face heated.

Then his tone turned from playful to serious. "But we are at a crossroads. We work for competing organizations, and we don't trust each other now. So let's just work together on this.

Find out what Victus is up to. Keep you safe. And then we'll never have to see each other again."

The problem was, I suddenly wasn't sure if that was what I wanted anymore.

LYRA

I tossed and turned in bed, unable to stop my brain from churning. How had I gotten here? How was this my life? One day, not so long ago, I'd gone to bed and everything had been relatively normal. I'd even had someone in my life for once.

Then the next day, everything had changed. I'd gone on a mission and shot my boyfriend. Or whatever he was.

And now you can't stop thinking about him.

I could practically *feel* him in the other room on watch. Making sure I was safe. The ever-present guardian.

From the moment we both learned the truth, Marcus had still kept an eye on me. First to see what I wanted with him, and then to save my life. I might have been angry with him, but I had to acknowledge that he had saved my life. More than once now. So it was hard to imagine that not even a full week ago, I had shot him.

And you can't get him out of your head now.

I kept thinking about every touch, every look, every nuanced kiss. I even played every date back on a mental reel trying to pinpoint the lies, where they were, how I'd missed them. I turned over again, adjusting my pillow and double-checking to make sure my weapon was there and loaded.

I didn't want to be caught off guard again.

You weren't even caught off guard then. They just sent six men to kill you. It took two of you to take them all down.

But the fact that I'd been surprised at all, that it hadn't even occurred to me that something like that *could* happen, that someone *could* get to me, shook me to my core.

Sure, in my line of work, you always knew you might die in the field. And maybe, just maybe, someone might get access to your information, but we were buried under so many layers of security that it was extremely unlikely. But still, I had been caught unaware, unprepared. Because I hadn't even thought it was a possibility. I'd let myself get complacent. Let myself believe that I couldn't be hit. Well, that was wrong. I had been targeted, so it was time to get my act together.

Why did I have Marcus on the brain? I should have been thinking about lots of other things. Who betrayed me, who was coming after me, all the things. Instead, my laser focus was pinned on one man. The way he made me feel and the way he made me ache. And the way he smelled. Like the ocean. Clean, crisp.

You want him.

I did. I wasn't going to lie to myself. There was no hiding it. I wanted to be with him. We were good together, but could I be with someone I couldn't trust? Maybe. I didn't know. I didn't know anything about him. Who he was, what he needed. He was a blank slate.

That's not true. You know him.

It didn't feel that way. The man in the other room had the smile of someone familiar, the laugh I'd grown to look forward to. But I didn't know him. How could I? Everything he'd ever told me was a fabrication.

Be real with yourself. Everything you told him was a lie too. So, how do you two be honest with each other?

Maybe starting with being honest about something that I wanted.

I tossed the covers off, unable to take it anymore. Was I going to do this?

You're a healthy woman, with a healthy libido. So it's

perfectly natural. Just go get what you want. And when you finally scratch the itch again, you can start thinking with your brain.

Maybe I just needed to get it out of my system.

Although, there was a small part of my brain willing and ready to call me out for my nonsense. I was telling myself that it would just be this one last time. Would it be though? Or would I just be weak again later and need his hands on me all over again.

In the end, I decided I didn't care.

I padded out into the living room, but something stopped me at the threshold. And it wasn't whether or not this was a bad idea as much as the constant, persistent thought of wondering if I had just been a mark to him. What if none of what I was feeling, none of that connection, was real?

Tyler really did a number on us, huh?

But after several deep breaths, I decided I didn't care. Marcus was here. He was the one on my mind. It didn't have to mean anything.

Uh-huh. Lies. All lies.

But I turned off that voice, opened the door, and walked through.

Marcus turned immediately with his gun at the ready. "What's wrong?"

"I couldn't sleep."

His gaze raked over me. I was wearing a lot more than the last time he'd seen me in bed clothes. This time my tank had a built-in bra, so at least my nips weren't going to make an appearance demanding his attention.

"I'll ask again. You can't sleep, so what's wrong?"

I licked my lips, unsure of what to say. "You were on my mind."

His gaze went instantly hooded. The corner of his lips

tugged up into a smile. "Is that right? I thought I was persona non grata."

Of course he would make me ask. He wasn't going to make this easy on me. "Lately I like you a lot better when you're not talking."

He grinned. "It's funny, but I like you a lot better when you *are*."

I stalked over to him, recognizing that each step took me further and further away from sanity and closer and closer to the point of no return. I knew I would face consequences. The thing was, I didn't care.

When I reached him, he holstered his weapon. "Lyra, you're looking at me with sin in your eyes. So I have to ask, are you sure you want to do this?"

I swallowed hard, meeting his deep blue gaze. "I still don't trust you."

He nodded and swallowed as he focused on my lips. "Right. But I'm going to repeat my question. So are you sure you want to do this?"

I nodded slowly. "I've decided I don't care."

"Fuck yes." He muttered as he turned and pulled me into his arms. And instead of quickly turning me around and slamming me against the door like I was prepared for, his free hand cupped my cheek, and his thumb smoothed over my cheekbone. "I know you don't trust me, but you can take me at my word. I'm not going to hurt you."

And then he slammed his lips on mine. Breaking that very promise with the searing burn of his kiss.

...

MARCUS

She was in my arms.

Just like I'd been imagining since that night on the floor in my old flat. Did she come to me because she wanted me, wanted what we had, that burning all-consuming fire? I could give that to her. I could give her more, too.

Except she was skittish.

But I was so desperate for her, that I wasn't sure how much gentleness I had in me. I wasn't sure how easy it would be to go slow.

Oh, we're not going slow.

Lyra took me by surprise, her tongue sliding over mine, her arms reaching up and looping around my neck. I knew taking her to the bedroom might not work. She wanted to keep things impersonal.

But I was going to show her that it didn't matter the location, didn't matter the time, the two of us were *always* going to be personal. Intimate. It was always going to mean something. I just needed her to catch on to that idea.

I lifted her easily, and she wrapped her legs around my waist. Our tongues slid over each other, a slide and retreat, a coaxing. A game. She made these little whimpering sounds at the back of her throat as my hands slid into her hair, anchoring her just how I needed her. She kept using her legs as leverage, trying to climb higher on my body. Trying to work her hips, her core, against the steel rod of my length.

I knew the layout of the room, so I made my way easily to the couch and avoided any major calamity without even having to break our kiss. Then I eased myself down with her on top of me. Once I sank down, she readjusted her legs so that she was braced on her knees, sitting on top of me. My hands settled onto her ass, bringing her over me in a slow, sliding ride.

We both moaned into each other's mouths as the friction lit us on fire.

Hell, if I'd have known it would be like this, I'd have been making out with her a lot more often. The grinding of her hips brought me closer and closer to her heat. I could feel her. She needed me just as much as I needed her.

Despite my attempts to take it slow, Lyra began to work herself faster, faster, and faster. When I dragged my lips back along her jaw, I said, "Slow down."

Her pants were harsh against the shell of my ear. "No, I don't want to."

"One of these days, you're going to learn to listen to me."

My hands clamped down on her hips tightly, and even though she fought me a little, I changed the cadence. Rolling her slowly. She gave me a low, frustrated whimper and then growled, "Hurry up."

"No. If you want to use me, you'll have to use me how *I* like."

"Asshole."

I grinned at that. "Oh, I'm pretty sure you like it like this too."

Staring into my eyes, she rocked on top of me, and I gazed down to the swell of her cleavage just over her tank top.

When I was certain she would adhere to the momentum rules, I eased up my grip on her hips, sliding my hands up under her tank and then helping her remove it. Sliding it up, up, up, showcasing the expanse of dark bronze skin glowing in the moonlight. And when I slid the tank up over her breasts, she hissed, and I moaned. Her tits were full and round. And they liked to point at me as if they were a beacon beckoning me home.

"God, your breasts are gorgeous."

I could hear the humor in her voice. "And they taste better than they look when you put your mouth around one of the nipples."

"You sure do love giving me directions."

"Stop arguing."

"Yeah, you know what, I might stop arguing, but I'm still going to do things my way."

I slid my hands up her rib cage and palmed both her

breasts, testing the weight, slowly rubbing my thumbs over her nipples, and she gave me a whimpering moan. "Marcus. Oh God."

"Yeah, love, you feel so good."

She kept writhing on me and at one point, I started to feel like my dick was wrestling for control of my mind.

The zinging sensations in my spine were a warning. Oh fuck, she was going to make me come like this.

Still cupping her breasts, I shifted my weight and gently turned her over so that I lay on top of her on the couch.

I settled my hips between hers, and she wrapped her legs around my waist again as we went back to kissing, sliding my tongue into her warm depths as one of my hands kept teasing her nipples, the other bracing myself above her so I didn't crush her.

I gave her nibbling kisses along her jaw, her neck. Inhaling deeply her scent of coconut and lime. Kissing down her clavicle and then the insides of her breasts.

She moaned. "Don't tease me, please. I'm begging you, Marcus."

"Oh God, yeah, I do love it when you beg."

Her hands tugged impatiently at my T-shirt, which I obliged by reaching behind my head and then pulling it up and over.

When I was bare chested, her brows lifted and her eyes gleamed. "That's better." Her hands reached up and slid up over my pecs, across my clavicle bone, over my shoulders and down, gently squeezing my biceps. "Pretty, so pretty."

I laughed softly then. "Glad you like what you see." From there it was the fight of who could touch more first. Nip here, slide a tongue over. She leaned up and grazed one of my nipples with her teeth. I thought that shocking volt of electricity was going to kill me. Incinerate me from the inside out. "Good God, woman."

She didn't let up though. She did it again and again, and it didn't matter how much I wanted control, how much I wanted to go slow. She was breaking me with exquisite torture, and she knew it.

I slid a hand into the bottom of her pajama shorts and into her panties, hesitating just for a moment as I lifted my gaze to hers and said, "Open wide."

"I'm pretty open now."

"Wider," I growled. When she did as I asked, I slid my finger gently over her clit, and her hips raised, trying to give me better access. But I wasn't giving her what she wanted exactly. Instead, I teased. The very tip of my middle finger circled her opening as I lifted my gaze to watch her reaction.

Her lips parted, her hips raised, her breasts thrust up in the sky, taunting me. She whispered, "Oh God. Oh please, don't play with me."

"Oh, sweetheart, we're barely getting started. I plan to play with you a lot."

Except the thing was, once I gently pushed with my middle finger and felt her inner walls tightly squeeze around that digit, my brain short-circuited.

It wasn't my fault. It can happen to anyone. But there went the last scraps of my control. The last threads of what I could do or think or say. And all I could think about was getting inside her. Making her ready, even wetter.

My finger slick, I stroked inside, slid out. Back inside, sliding out again. When I retreated, she gasped and reached for me. "No. Don't stop."

Smiling down on her, I slid in two fingers. Stretching her, making her ready.

Her fingers dug into my shoulders. "Marcus please, please, please, please, we can go slow later. I promise. Can we just... faster."

"Are you sure? Because I plan to tease you for hours. Like you've been doing to me."

"I haven't been teasing you. Marcus, I'm sorry, I'm sorry, you can tease me later, please, please, please."

I liked her begging. I liked her wet. I liked the way that she clawed at my shoulders. I liked the way she panted my name. I wanted it all.

The more she writhed, the more I took. Adding my thumb to the mix, always keeping her just on the edge. "Is that what you want? Faster?" And then I eased my fingers out of her, reaching for her shorts and her panties and tugging them down in one swift yank.

As she gasped, I gave her no time. I dove in. My hands on her arse, my shoulders very deliberately widening her thighs. And I licked. A firm stroke from her ass to the top of her clit. And then I fastened my mouth around her clit and sucked.

Her gasping scream was all the encouragement I needed. She writhed in my arms. "Oh my God. Oh my God. Holy cow. Marcus, please, wow." And then her hands were in my hair. That stinging burn of her tugging on my scalp made me grin as I hummed a little. Lyra thrashed in my arms, her hips gyrating. Her juices running over my tongue, my face, my lips. Oh, but I wasn't done. I gently released her clit only to slide down an inch and use my tongue on her just like I'd used my fingers. Fucking her gently, stroking her. Worshiping her pussy like I should have always.

And with my thumb I stroked over her clit again and again and again. Her legs quivered, and I could feel them clamping around my head and my shoulders until she had me locked in place.

The tighter she squeezed, the more I licked and fucked her.

Her hips raised off the couch, and she must've been gripping onto the armrest because she kept screaming, "Marcus. Marcus, oh my God."

It was only as she eased down that I pulled back even remotely.

As I sat back, she lay limp, her legs still wide open, teasing me, taunting me. Lyra's eyes fluttered closed, and the look on her face was pure splendor.

I loved putting that look on her face. And I planned to do it again.

When I stood, she whimpered. "You're not done here."

All I could do was laugh. "Oh, trust me. You need a break, and I'm most certainly not done." She lifted her lids and watched me warily.

When I unsnapped the top button of my jeans, her lips lifted into an impish smile. "That's more like it."

"Oh, is this you thinking you're in control now?"

She drew her legs together and I frowned. "No, I want them open."

"Well, for what I had in mind, that position's awkward."

"We're not done here, Lyra."

"Who said anything about being done?"

As I reached for my zipper, her fingers reached out to help me. She shoved my jeans and boxers down over my hips and then licked her lips as she sat forward. Just watching that small motion, my whole body went to steel. Oh God. She was in charge. And she knew it.

She leaned forward and, with the tip of her tongue, licked my dick from the tip to the base.

I was completely helpless to do anything other than drop my head back and moan out, "Fuck."

Then I could feel her fingers wrap around the base, and I dared a look down, praying to God I didn't just come all over her face.

Then she shifted again. Driving me insane, she knew what she was doing. Knew she was teasing me, torturing me, as she sat back and winked, and I knew I was toast. She was doing this on purpose. Fucking with me. Trying to make me lose my goddamn mind.

"Lyra, I'm—" She wasn't listening. She wrapped her lips around the head of my dick and sucked, her tongue playing with the underside just enough to make my knees buckle. I reached out and slid my hands into her hair. Holding her still. "Behave."

Around the head of my dick, she grinned and then took all of me in, deep throating me, and I let out another extended curse. "Jesus fucking Christ. Lyra. Oh fuck. Fuck me."

And then she owned me. She stroked from the base to tip and back again in slow rhythmic motion. And I could feel it again, the hum of my spine, blistering heat coming from me. "Lyra."

She shook her head, letting me know she was continuing.

I wanted to be inside her.

"Lyra. I'm going to come."

She only sucked harder. Worked her hand faster. Brought her other hand down to my balls and squeezed them gently.

"Fuck me, fuck, fuck, fuck."

I tried to think of anything to stop a barreling orgasm from coming for me. Only by sheer force of will did I pull her away. Then I tipped her head back. "You are a naughty girl."

"I was busy."

"Oh, now I'm gonna get busy."

I reached for my wallet and grabbed a condom before shuffling off my jeans. I was sheathed in seconds and threw her back on the couch, gently but forcefully enough that she knew I meant business. I grabbed her one leg and dangled it over the couch the way it had been when I'd had her on my tongue. And then I gripped at her inner thighs, opening her up just enough.

Her gaze was on me. Dark eyes intent, hot. Searing. "Marcus. Yes."

I guided my dick to her, watching as I breached her entrance ever so slightly.

Her gaze on mine, mine on hers, we were locked, watching each other. And then I slammed home. Her screaming cry of, "Yes," was what I wanted to hear. I pulled nearly all the way back out and then slid home again.

She gave me a low, moaning groan. "Yes. God, yes. Oh my God." One of my thumbs gave a hard press to her clit over and over again in those tight, tight circles that she liked so much. She squeezed my dick with her inner muscles like a vice grip. But I didn't let up my retreat and slide. And before I knew it, she screamed my name, head thrown back, breasts tipped up, hips grinding on mine. Blistering, searing heat came from me, starting with my toes and traveling like a rocket throughout my body, so fast it surprised me, instantly blinding me in bright white light as I came. All I heard as unconsciousness nearly took me was my name on her lips. "My Marcus."

9

MARCUS

Last night was a mistake.

A hot mistake.

A mistake none the less. I knew what it meant to me. But she'd made it clear that what happened last night was sex and nothing more as far as she was concerned. Once we found out what was going on at The Firm and made sure she was safe, she was determined to shut me out forever.

I shoved those thoughts aside. I had a mission. A plan to execute. And this was not a plan Lyra was going to like.

We had moved to a new temporary safe house last night. She was already on the mend. And even if she was in pain after last night, there was no way she was letting me know it. She had this way of blocking it out. I could see it now that I was aware of the signs. Her strength had always attracted me to her, even before I knew the depth of it.

I glanced over at her meditating on the living room rug.

Dangerous. I dragged my eyes back to my computer monitor where they needed to be, not on her arse. Though, bloody hell, what a spectacular arse it was. I couldn't even believe that my feelings toward her had been tempered on our first two dates. But obviously, she wasn't interested in moving forward, so I reminded myself for the tenth time that day not to be an idiot.

All morning, I'd been looking for a way into the Victus weapon sale. Lyra didn't know I had reached out to Rhodes yet. But unlike her team, mine *could* be trusted. Would she see it that way?

I wasn't sure how Maggie or Michael were going to deal with it, but we needed backup, and her friend Addie just wasn't enough. But at least I could spin it as trying to hunt down Victus by pretending I was using a civilian to get us in.

The house of cards you're building will topple.

Maybe, but I had to get Victus off her arse. I couldn't let it go. I couldn't walk away from her and hope that somehow she'd survive. I had to do something.

"Are you going to keep staring at my ass, or are you going to tell me what you're doing on the computer?"

I bit down on the inside of my cheek to keep from smirking.

"I'm doing both. Which would you like me to answer first? Your arse is spectacular. But you know that, which is why you turned your mat purposely so you could taunt me."

"If you feel taunted, it's not my fault."

"Are you sure? Because it feels like it is."

"Okay, let's try a different route. What are you working on?"

"Right now, I'm trying to get us into that Victus bidding game for the weapon."

She turned. The sports bra and leggings that she was wearing were simplistic, yet eye-catching. I'd told Addie to go for understated when she provided us supplies. But if this was understated, I was a goner. Little mesh cut-outs showed me just a hint of under-boob, just a strip of stomach, enough to make me salivate, but not enough to be too showy. It was like she was deliberately trying to torture me. "And? Can we get in?"

"I'm reaching out to a few contacts."

She lifted her brow. "And by contacts, you mean your team?"

I could lie. I could tell her that no, of course not. I wouldn't endanger her life that way. But I was done lying. "Yes. My team isn't trying to get me killed."

She ground her teeth. "I'm not working with Exodus."

"You don't have to. I do suggest you work with *me* though, because I'm currently the only one trying to save your delectable arse."

"You have your own reasons, I think."

"I do. Besides, where my superiors are concerned, I've stated that I'm using a civilian. I'm not compromising you."

Her brow pinched just slightly, letting me know that she was pondering this. Wondering why I was cutting her slack. "Why are you protecting me?"

"Again, if you don't know that by now, I can't help you."

"Right. Fine. Are you able to do it? Get us into that meeting?"

I nodded. "Of course, I am. You're not going to like the cover though."

"Oh God, why do I already regret agreeing to working together?"

"You have a healthy sense of self-preservation. But I'm all you've got, so suck it up. We have transport and a way into the auction. I'm going in as Klaus Rangoon, a German arms dealer. And you, my dear, will be my lover/bodyguard."

Her brows lifted and her mouth twitched. "Does Klaus need a bodyguard?"

"Guard his body in all kinds of ways."

"Who is Klaus anyway?"

"An arms dealer who actually did get in on the Victus

bidding, but he's one of ours. He's notoriously reclusive. There have been several different deals over the years where we've been able to use him."

"That's not bad."

"Thanks. I'll be sure to tell Michael and Maggie that."

"Who are they?"

I nodded slightly. "Michael and Maggie are handlers. Michael runs this section of Exodus. Maggie is the number two. More like the brains and the heart, I guess."

"Wow, okay. And why do you make that face when you say Maggie's name?"

I frowned. "I didn't make a face, did I? No face."

"Yes, you made a face. It's almost like you don't want to say her name. Ah, is she an ex?"

I shook my head. "No, not an ex. Sometimes I think she wants to be, but it never happened."

"Oh." She furrowed her brow then. Her lips slightly pinched, and I recognized that face. The one that said she most certainly wanted to kill something.

"Relax. Maggie's fine. And after Simone, I wouldn't be with anyone at work."

"Aren't you breaking that rule with me?"

"Technically, I don't work with you. And we are no longer a thing, remember?"

"Oh, I remember. Just once, I'd like to have a normal boyfriend. One who does not kill people for a living."

I chuckled at that. "You'd be bored with that person. Someone who comes home every night for dinner at six. Attentive, boring, borrows the neighbor's lawn mower, wears a lot of khakis. Not for you, right?"

She wrinkled her nose. "Why would I go with the khakis? Maybe I want someone who has a little style."

I glanced down at myself. "I can have style when I want."

She's not talking about you specifically, knob. Besides, you know better.

I did. The danger of what she did, of what *we* did... I couldn't do that again. Besides, we'd both been clear that it was a one-time thing. Just a way to scratch an itch.

Shaking off those thoughts, I smirked and said, "So, what do you say, bodyguard? Have you thought of all the different ways that you can guard my body yet?"

She laughed at that. The sound was light and effervescent, almost enough to buoy the dark mood that was weighing us both down.

"God, you've been dying to bust that one out, haven't you?"

I grinned. "Okay, fine, I have. Come on, it's funny."

"Yeah, sure. What are the details?"

"We are off to Latvia. Wheels up tonight."

"What are we doing until tonight?" she asked with no hint of suggestion in her tone.

My gaze slid over her body. My body tightened thinking about all the different types of things that we could get up to before tonight. "We'll get supplies, and you'll need new clothes."

She frowned. "Addie already sent clothes."

"No, if you're going to be my bodyguard, you'll need to dress the part."

"Oh, let me guess, leather, black, slinky?"

"Well, slinky, yes. Leather, no. We're going to need to find you a ball gown that will conceal your weapon."

She lifted a brow. "Oh, no. Please tell me we're not going shopping."

I grinned at her. "Oh yes, we're going shopping."

LYRA

The dress we picked for me was slinky. I knew that one wrong move and there might be a wardrobe malfunction. It was braless and had a slit so high my vajayjay was almost on full display for the world to see, no dinner required first. Although I did feel sexy, and I had a thigh holster, so bonus. My diamond necklace doubled as a camera, and I had my hair pins that I could use to build a knife.

After the plane landed, we went to the hotel to get dressed. It took me a little bit to get ready. I stepped out into the room, waiting for Marcus to look up. He took so long, I cleared my throat. "Ahem."

His gaze slid up from his monitor, to my face, down to my toes, and then slowly back up again.

But all he said was, "Good, you're dressed."

I blinked at him. "What? Even I know I look good."

He smirked. "No one's saying you don't look good. But we're strictly business, remember?"

"Ah, way to be a dick."

"You were the one who wanted this."

He stood, and I got the full picture. Jesus Christ, he had on tuxedo pants, a crisp white Tom Ford shirt, and his cuff links were silver and diamonds, intertwined. Understated, but still expensive as hell. He pushed his seat back and then reached for his jacket. Dear fucking Lord, he was... Wow. "Not bad."

He grinned then. "Wow, you sure know how to one-up my praise. That was effusive." He shook his head. "But, sure. I'll take it. Are you ready?"

I nodded. "Walk me through it again. No fuck-ups."

He laughed. "I'm not the fuck up."

"Well, to be fair, we haven't worked together before. So let's go through the plan one more time."

He sighed. "Turn up at the event. Drink nothing. Eat nothing. Your rule."

"You'd be surprised how many times I've been drugged."

He blinked at that. "What?"

"The worst was this Ukrainian who liked to collect women for his harem. Granted, I knew what I was doing undercover, but still, it was awful. Shaking those drugs off, even with my training? It was hard to get my brain back online."

"All right. Show up. IDs. You'll have to hand over your weapons, but obviously you are well skilled at hand-to-hand. We'll go in, catch the players, get the photographs, and you'll stay close to me, obviously. There shouldn't be anyone there who can identify you. We'll be fine. Trust me."

"Trust you?"

He smirked. "My team will be there. As far as they're concerned, you're a civilian, so your safety is at the top of their list of things to do."

"Forgive me if I can't trust people I don't know, all right?"

"You can trust me, though, right?"

I wanted to tell him that, no, I could not trust him. But I knew now that I could. Whether I liked it or not, he had saved my life. He had come into a situation that wasn't of his own making, and he'd kept me safe. I didn't want to think about it, but I might have died on my own against six agents. Life had turned out nasty. "Yeah, I trust you."

"You and I are only there to tag them. Any players that we see. Everything else, we leave to my team."

"We need that weapon."

"My team will grab it."

I shook my head. "No, if we see it, we have to take it."

"We'll see if the opportunity presents itself, but our main job is to tag."

I wasn't a fan of this plan. "No, I don't like it."

"This is the plan we have. Suck it up, love."

"Are you always this forceful? In charge? I like you less now."

He grinned. "I'm pretty sure you like me *more*."

I wanted to hit him. "Fine, are you ready?"

He swung his tux jacket on, double-checking if everything was in place. I smoothed out his lapels, and his gaze raked over mine as I did so. "Yeah, I guess I'm ready. I'm not going to let anything happen to you, Lyra."

"And I won't make anything happen to you. We're connected now."

"We are. And just so you remember, we're taking the members of Victus alive."

I blinked at him. "Oh, goddamn it. Did Addie tell you?"

His grin flashed. "I didn't really take you as one for bag-and-kill."

"He was a human trafficker. You kill one guy, one time, and no one ever lets you forget."

He was still chuckling as we walked out the door, and there was something about this feeling of belonging that I wanted to hold on to. I just hoped to Christ that I wasn't making a mistake by trusting him.

10

MARCUS

As it turned out, I didn't need to worry about Lyra. She was, as she'd said, very good at her job. She used some kind of pins or something to put her hair up, showcasing her elegantly long neck. But as she'd shown me on the elevator on the way up here, those pins, when locked together, formed an excellent knife.

"Wow."

"Let's just say that female Valentine ops get patted down a lot for weapons."

Her just saying that made me choke a little, and I asked the question automatically. "Have you ever been a Valentine op?"

Her eyes went wide. "No, not me. I lack the requisite skill set."

I frowned at that, knowing that we'd been combustible together. "What does that mean?"

"I'm not sexy enough."

All I could do was blink at her as we paced around the room that we'd been shown to wait in before entering the party. Her dress showcased her perfect arse, as well as her long, lithe legs. The heels alone... God, what I could do with her naked wearing just those heels. How was she not sexy?

"I'm sorry. I'm confused."

"You're good for my ego, but I don't have that thing that oozes sex appeal. I think it's that I have a very no-nonsense general attitude to me. Addie was a Valentine op for a while. She finally got transferred out. I think she's a lot happier now."

I shook my head. "Jesus."

"Oh, don't go feeling bad for them. Some operatives love it. The detachment, the lack of emotional connection, they can do it easily. I'm just not one of those people. And I think after a while, it also took its toll on Addie."

"Right."

She frowned. "Don't you have Valentine ops?"

I shook my head. "No, we don't. We don't require any of our female agents to, you know..." My voice trailed.

She lifted the corner of her lips. "Oh wow, don't tell Addie, I feel like she'd be rushing to join up on principle alone."

"Is it a requirement at The Firm?"

She shook her head. "No, but if you're young, beautiful, and ooze that kind of sex appeal that Addie does, it becomes one of your top options. Addie never said that she felt she had to, but I get the impression that sometimes she did."

"Let me guess, no male Valentine ops?"

She laughed then. "Actually, there are. Tyler was one of them."

I ground my teeth. "Right. He was supposed to show you the ropes."

"Yeah, and make me believe it. Anyway, it doesn't matter now."

No, what mattered was I wanted to kill the guy.

The exterior of the building we were in had looked like some kind of Greek Villa on Mykonos. Brilliant white that shone like a diamond on the horizon. The holding room we'd initially been placed in was more of an office area. While elegant and modern, it was, by and large, understated.

A banging sound echoed from the door. When we opened it, a man so large he blocked any light coming through the door stood in front of us. I didn't like it, but Lyra stood in front of me, playing the part of my bodyguard. "What do you want?"

"Time for bidding. Follow me."

He stepped aside, and I followed behind Lyra, enjoying the view. Her dress was nearly backless, covering just the top of her arse. Her heels made a *click-clack* sound on the marble floor as we walked. The further we went from the offices, the more opulent and gilded the furnishings became. There was more rare art, more brocade tapestries, as if suddenly we'd stepped into Versailles or something.

Adrenaline was already spiking in my blood. My team knew that we wouldn't be able to have comm units, but the tracking chip I wore inside my tuxedo also served as a communication device in case of emergency. It was small, but it definitely served its purpose. It was enough for me, since I already knew that they were out there. I'd wondered about Lyra and that comment she'd made about not having a team she could trust. I knew she meant Tyler. What I gathered was that there was something more to that story. I knew she'd felt betrayed because she'd fallen for him, but there was definitely more than that.

We were led into a large receiving room. Gilded opulence was the motif with sculptural moldings and expensive-looking art. Pockets of people stood around the room.

Light from the massive crystal chandelier hanging above set the room a glitter. All around, waiters in tails served champagne and caviar. Whitestop, the group behind the sale, had spared no expense.

Very slowly and deliberately, we glanced around at each and every person, making sure our cameras caught them. Hers in her necklace, mine in my cufflink, putting a facial tag on each of them. None of them would be able to walk out of there without Exodus agents all over them. No one approached anyone else. No one spoke to anyone. We were all too busy sizing each other up. When Mads McLean walked into the room, I tensed. It was unlikely that he would recognize me, but Lyra had mentioned that she *had* fought him, so it was likely he might recognize her.

He hadn't looked in her direction yet, though. I whispered to Lyra, "Is he going to be a problem for you?"

"Maybe. I'll try not to let him get a direct line of sight on me."

Mads stood at the front of the room. "Friends, thank you all for joining us. As you know, my associates and I have been working on this little party for some time. Thank you for placing your bids. The seller, however, wanted to meet with each and every one of you because they want to know the people they're doing business with. You understand, of course."

Fuck.

Next to me, Lyra tensed, but her face remained placid and cool. She still kept her body at an angle, just in case. "This wasn't part of the plan." Her voice was tight.

"You have to be willing to improvise," I muttered.

"If we get in there, and Stannis Prochenko is there, we're made. He most certainly saw us."

"I know. Let's just see what happens. I don't have the schematics, but my people are here. There will be a way out. Trust me."

"You can't just tell me to trust you."

"That's what we've got right now."

And that *was* all we had. I made two taps on my audio unit to make sure Rhodes was receiving on the other end.

"Whitestop is on site. I repeat, Whitestop is on site. Negative on the visual."

One by one, I watched the other buyers stroll over to Mads McLean's side of the room, and I bit my tongue. "This isn't looking good."

"You're telling me?" Lyra glanced around then pulled the pins from her hair, letting it spill over her shoulders. Surreptitiously, she assembled her weapon.

"Stay cool." As we approached, Mads was making his way toward us. As he got closer, I turned Lyra suddenly and planted a soft kiss on her lips. When I pulled back, I counted slowly to ten until Mads walked by us. Then sadly, I released her.

Slightly dazed, she frowned up at me. "What are you doing?"

I simply said, "Mads," as a means of explanation.

"Jesus." She dragged in a deep breath of relief.

As we stepped into the room, she frowned. There was Guzin Kola, number two at Whitestop. He'd been on our list for a long time. I made the visual tag so my team would know that he was there.

He smiled at the two of us. "I heard that you are Klaus Rangoon, but you haven't told me who your lovely associate is."

Lyra stepped forward, brows drawn down. "Who's asking?"

Kola grinned. "Ah, a bit of spice. I always like that myself. Step forward, we'll need your thumbprint to verify you are who you say you are."

I stepped forward with absolute confidence and then very carefully slid my thumb into the pocket-sized device he had.

Several seconds passed, and the dial spun and spun and spun. Kola smiled at me, and the man next to him with the gun stepped forward. Which made Lyra step forward.

She, as far as they were concerned, had no weapon. Kola

turned his smile on her. "Ah, little one, you're going to tear my men apart with your bare hands to protect your man? Where do I get one of you?"

"I'm not for sale," she ground out.

He laughed. "Ah, my darling, that's where you're wrong. *Everyone* is for sale."

"Not me."

"Would you care to see how much your man here would charge me for you?"

I smiled down at Lyra. "She's not for sale."

Kola grinned down at her menacingly. "Oh, in that case, I will either have to charm you or take you for myself. Which shall it be?"

Her gaze slid over him inch by inch. "Neither. You wouldn't survive the night."

Kola chuckled. "Ugh, I do envy you for a woman like this. I have heard that black women are so much feistier in the sack. Are they?"

I ground my teeth, tamping down my urge to put my fist in his face. "Can we get this show on the road?"

He raised his hands. "Okay, okay. I didn't mean to cause offense."

Next to me, I could feel Lyra vibrating, and I prayed to God she was going to be able to hold it together for the rest of this.

"I see you've made your bid. I do regret to inform you that—"

Before he could finish, I stepped forward. "Let's not do this little play where you act like you can drive up the price. I know I have the highest bid."

He smiled at me. "There's no way you can know that."

I smiled as I recalled the information Curtis had given me right before we entered the party. He had one of our hackers working just off site so he could get past the firewalls. "All right, the Italians offered $7.2 million. The New Masons offered $7.5 million. Shall I continue?"

Kola's skin went pale. "How do you know this?"

"I told you. I know things. Let's not play any more games. I offered you the highest bid. Now, either you like money or you don't. But I'm not here to play if you don't like money. We'll be on our way before you waste any more of my time."

His gaze narrowed. "You think you're smarter than everyone, don't you?"

"It pays to be smarter than everyone. Then you don't get cheated."

Kola stepped forward, and Lyra stepped in front of me, playing her role to the letter.

His man stepped up to Lyra and then made the mistake of putting his hand on her arm.

Lyra glanced at it, glanced up at him, and then smiled. The move she executed was so quick, with her hand on his, and a twist of her body, she quickly turned until she had him coming down to his knees with full access and control of his wrist. Kola smiled and clapped. "Wow. God. Are you sure she's not for sale?"

"No. And I'm growing impatient. Either the weapon is mine, or it's not."

He nodded slowly. "Fine, fine. Let's not get testy. You are indeed the highest bidder." He gave me a card. "It's at the docks. I assume you have your own people ready. Have them call this number. As soon as the money is transferred of course."

I glanced at Lyra. She released his guard and put her hands up, showing she was no longer a threat.

Kola narrowed his gaze at her. "Have I seen you before? I would swear I have. But God, I would remember a creature such as yourself."

Everything this guy said to her was meant to be somehow flattering, but instead, it was disgusting and full of mockery.

"No." She kept her voice guttural. Low. Unrecognizable.

"If you're certain, my darling." He turned back to me. "Here's the account number. Please type it in."

As I typed in the account number, my team could also see the numbers. The money would appear there, and then we would have exactly one minute to get the hell out of Dodge because that money would have vanished.

"The numbers are typed in."

He grinned and clapped. "Ah, excellent."

He had his men verify and then nodded. "Here is your card. I assume your people will be standing by."

I made the call and then rattled the information off.

"Pleasure doing business. I do hope to do business with you again, Klaus."

We'd just turned to go when Kola called out to Lyra. "My darling, just know that I'll be seeing you very, very soon."

Lyra faltered, but then she kept moving. She walked in front of me again, and when we stepped out of the room, all hell broke loose.

LYRA

The power was cut, and somewhere in the distance, glass shattered.

What the fuck? My first thought was someone was raiding the auction.

I hadn't intended to *actually* have to protect Marcus. It hadn't really been part of the plan. Obviously, he could protect himself, but goddamn.

Marcus's hand wrapped around mine, and we hustled out.

People were running and screaming. I heard gunshots, and my blood chilled.

We busted out of the meeting room toward our egress route.

Down the hall, bright lights shone, and I dragged Marcus with me. The gunshots that shattered the plaster walls around us barely missed us. Jesus Christ.

We could see the shooter who waited for us, and I held my breath. He moved with a cat-like grace, and something made me pause. Why were his movements so memorable to me?

Marcus tried to stop me. Suddenly, the scope turned our direction. The light on the end illuminated my face. There was no mistaking who I was, and the man in the hall froze. Then he cursed.

"Lyra? What the fuck are you doing here?" Tyler asked as he ripped his mask off.

"I could ask you the same question."

Behind me, Marcus cursed too. "Jesus fucking Christ. Is The Firm here?" He tried to tug me down the hall.

Tyler shook his head. "You can't go that way." He pointed toward our egress route.

"What do you mean?" I frowned.

"Don't fucking go that way."

"What are you doing? I don't trust you."

"Right now, sweetheart, the feeling is mutual. But do yourself a favor, and for once in your goddamn life, listen to me."

I expected him to shoot, to take me out, take out Marcus. But nothing happened. He just moved on.

Marcus grabbed my hand and we tried to head back toward our egress point, but more bullets came at us.

"I thought I was fucking clear," Tyler said. "If you want to fight a whole handful of Firm agents, go that way. Fine. Don't listen to me. But I'll tell you now, it's not going to end well for you."

Marcus looked at me. "We have an alternate route."

I had no recourse but to follow him. Tyler grabbed Marcus's arm. "I already told you, you're going to get killed if you go that way."

"What is your fucking problem, mate?"

"Both of you stop it," I said. "We have trouble. So maybe we all get the fuck out of here and then figure out what we've got later?"

I could feel Marcus's tension.

But I didn't have time to fight with him right now.

Tyler led us up one hall and then down another.

"Where's the team?" I asked.

"They're trying to capture Guzin Kola so that they can intercept the weapon. You're not supposed to be here."

"Leave it alone." I muttered.

He grabbed my arm and dragged me against him. In a low voice, he asked, "What the fuck is he doing here?"

I swallowed hard. "Not your business."

"It is if…"

His eyes suddenly went wide. "He's Exodus."

"You know what? I don't even have to explain myself to you."

"You do when you're interrupting a mission."

"You should have called it in by now, Tyler. Why haven't you?"

"Shut the fuck up."

"Wait. Because you're doing something you're not supposed to be doing right now too. So my question is, what the fuck is it?"

Marcus said, "If you two can drop your lover's spat, we have actual work to do."

When we hit what would have been one of our alternate

targets for egress, we started to duck in. Tyler stopped us though. "Where the fuck do you think you're going?"

Marcus laughed. "Oh, did you think we only had one way out of here? No. You're not stopping us from leaving."

"I need to take you back to headquarters. Keep her out of fucking trouble. I can cover for you."

I frowned. "You recognize I don't trust you to cover for anything, right?"

He glowered at me. "For fuck's sake Lyra, you're about to get yourself killed."

"No, I'm not."

I turned to go with Marcus, and Tyler clamped a hand on mine. "No. You're staying with me."

Marcus didn't like that. "Let her go. In matters like this when there is danger to civilian life, I'm in charge of her now. You might even think I'm her daddy." And then Marcus swung a fist.

Tyler was surprised, but he recovered quickly enough to hit Marcus on his jaw.

And then they were trading punches back and forth. Both of them swinging.

Shit. "We don't have fucking time for this."

Kicks. Blocks.

Tyler glowered at me. "If you go with him, I can't protect you."

"You were never protecting me in the first place."

"Lyra, we have to go," Marcus said.

While there was no love lost between us, Tyler represented everything about who I thought I was. If he went back to The Firm with this information, I was done. My whole life would explode.

11

LYRA

As it turned out, Tyler was right. If we'd gone the way we had planned to, we would have run straight into Firm agents. From our vantage point at the top of the hill, I looked down through the binoculars and could see them.

Marcus said, "We should go this way, down the embankment. Make a right. We can still rendezvous with my team."

"He *was* trying to help us."

His voice was terse when he spoke. "Now is not the time. Can you worry about your boyfriend, you know, when we're out of here?"

"That's not even fair."

"I don't really care about fair right now."

"Fine." I followed him down the embankment. The slit in my dress was coming in handy, but my heels were slowing us down some.

"Are you okay?" Marcus asked.

"I'm fine."

"Jesus Christ, Lyra. Come here. I'll carry you."

I scowled at him and slapped at his hands. "I don't need you *to carry* me."

"You clearly do. The way you're going, we don't have time for that."

"If you carry me, I'd flatten you. Besides, there's no need," I scoffed.

He rolled his eyes. "Is this what's going to happen, you know, every time we need to do something? We're going to argue about it, then we're going to fight, then we're going to fuck? Because if that's the way everything is going to end, I'm here for it. But in the interest of time, maybe we could speed up this process."

"We are not going to fuck."

"Ah, there she is. I get you, but this is faster. Besides, I'd qualify last night as a fuck. I promise next time will be slow and sweet."

I dragged off the heels and pulled out the foldable slippers I'd stuffed in my garters. "First of all, I come prepared for every occasion. Second of all, there won't be a next time."

Lies.

He blinked at me in surprise. "Yes, there will be. And that," he indicated my shoes, "was impressive."

"Not my first rodeo. Let's go."

My feet felt infinitely better in the flats. These shoes weren't sturdy or meant for fast movements, but they were certainly better than heels or bare feet.

Down the embankment, as we were trying to stay out of sight, I saw two of my agents making the runs. I wanted to jump out. I wanted to scream, 'Hey guys, it's me. I'm here. I'm one of you.' But I knew that wasn't going to work. At the moment, I wasn't one of them. I was not on their team right now.

Somehow, that revelation hurt. It shouldn't have, but it still stung. When we made it to the main road, Marcus nodded his head. "Okay, just over there, Rhodes is waiting. Check your surroundings and then get across as soon as you—"

As he was talking, my gaze shifted just for a moment, and then I saw the red pinpoint of a sniper scope on his chest. I didn't even think about it. I tossed myself in front of him and shoved him to the ground, using the full weight of my body. My people were firing on me?

You don't know if they're your people anymore.

Footsteps were coming toward us quickly. Marcus rolled us over, pulling us to a crouch as he growled, "Run."

There was no checking for cover. All we could do was lay cover fire across the road and book it. Because behind us, we had trouble incoming.

"Friends of yours?" he asked.

"They don't know it's me they're shooting at."

We ducked and used the spindly trees for the bullshit cover that they were, but it wasn't enough.

"Are you sure?"

"I don't need this from you right now, Marcus."

"Do you still want to tell me how noble your team is? How great they are?"

"Shut it."

Someone fired from the left. Marcus hit the target easily. The target went down and then Marcus went over to him.

"What are you doing?"

He held up the walkie-talkie and the gun the guy had been carrying.

We booked it across, and when I fired, I aimed to fire at their feet. Because the last thing I wanted to do was hit a teammate.

Except, they're not treating you like a teammate.

It sucked being uncertain.

Just as we hit the edge of the tree line, I turned and saw the standard uniforms of Victus. I breathed a sigh of relief.

My guys weren't shooting at us. Those weren't our

uniforms. And this time, I felt zero guilt when I aimed my gun higher. I hit my target square in the chest.

Marcus turned, saw my hit, and nodded. "Nice shot."

"Well, it's easier to shoot someone when you know they're not yours."

I went to grab his gun in case any of his little friends came for him too. And then I heard it on the walkie-talkie Marcus had picked up.

"Someone give me a confirmation on Lyra Wilkinson. She's the target. Out."

I froze, sure that I couldn't have heard that right. Sure that it was a mistake. How the hell was I in the target package?

Marcus wouldn't let me stop though, dragging me with him as if I'd never slowed down. "You don't have time for this."

But I'd already heard it. Someone was coming for me. Whoever they were, they wanted me dead. And I had no idea why.

Unless...

Tyler.

He'd told them I was here.

MARCUS

LYRA HAD BEEN quiet since returning to the safe house. There wasn't much I could say to make her feel better. There was no agony aunt advice for situations like this. As expected, my team had been waiting with a ride out of there, but they delivered bad news too.

Someone had beaten us to the weapon. Rhodes said there had been a short and nasty firefight, so our little mission was not exactly a rousing success.

And watching Lyra in bits was killing me. Someone was

most certainly trying to kill her. The question was if it was someone from her own team.

Not that I gave a rat's arse about her feelings.

Liar. You love her.

I had told myself that I didn't want anyone else after Simone, that I couldn't love anyone else after her. But that was a lie, obviously, because I had fallen for Lyra. Even though I didn't want to. She was supposed to be fun as opposed to being a distraction. As opposed to blowing my cover.

But still, I'd ended up falling for her in the kind of way that filled me with fear that someone was coming after her. The kind of way that made me distracted because I wanted to kill them. It had taken over the mission directive in my brain.

Annihilate anyone who wanted to cause her pain.

By the time she made it out of the bath and came out with a tightly cinched robe, she looked slightly less shell-shocked. "Thanks."

"For what?"

"You know, your team, getting us out of there. I'm sorry I hesitated. I don't know what happened."

"You just found out that someone is deliberately trying to kill you."

"Not *someone*. Tyler."

Just hearing the guy's name had me grinding my teeth, but I wasn't convinced she was right. "To what purpose? It doesn't make any sense. He helped us get out and then helped Victus try to kill us? Why?"

"I don't know." She buried her face in her hands, and I could tell the confusion and frustration was eating away at her.

"Well, you said things didn't end well between you. I mean, what happened?"

"Honestly, we just broke up. There was nothing nefarious behind it. There's no reason for him to come after me. No reason to hate me. It just doesn't connect, but his return to LA at the same time Victus showed up is just too coincidental. It doesn't jive."

My brow furrowed. "You can't give me a single reason he'd be out to get you?"

She shook her head. "Look, when we broke up, he was the one who dumped me. We had no reason to be on each other's radar. It just doesn't make sense."

"Okay. Then let's get some rest. We'll figure it out in the morning."

She dug her hands into her hair. "There's no way I'm sleeping with all these questions running through my head. I've been through it a million times. You're right. He helped us."

"All right, then who else might be calling the shots?"

She ran a hand through her damp curls.

"Shit. I didn't get you a shower cap." I'd meant to pack one for her.

"It's okay. Tomorrow, it'll just dry out bigger. I have some products in my bag, so I'll put some conditioner on it. Hopefully it won't be too crazy."

"I should have remembered. I'm sorry."

She gave me the softest smile with a little peek of a dimple, and a swift rush of blood warmed my body. "You saved my life already tonight. Well, honestly, two nights ago as well. I don't expect you to also save my hair."

I cleared my throat. "Right."

"But, before we go on, I want to apologize."

I frowned. "For what?"

"Before, when I said that you... us, it wasn't real. I was pissed off. Angry. You put yourself in danger because of me, and I'm not even sure I deserve that."

"Don't be ridiculous. Of course, you deserve that. You know how I feel about you."

Her gaze lifted and met mine. "There is a part of me that doesn't entirely believe it or trust it."

"Well, you should."

She nodded. "Yeah, I absolutely should."

"Okay, so what are we going to do?"

"You mean, besides getting some rest? Nothing."

"Lyra, we have to come down from this. We can't think if we're in a constant state of adrenaline all the time."

"I know. I want my life back. My people. They're the only family I have left."

I wrapped my arms around her. "Hey, stop. Worrying about whether or not your team is trying to have you killed is not at all helpful. Let's just focus on what we know, okay?" I went over to the liquor cabinet, pleased to find some whiskey in there, and poured us both a glass. "I don't know how good this stuff is, but it will calm the nerves."

She took it with a smile. "Thanks."

She lifted the glass and drained it quickly.

I chuckled. "Maybe slow down just a little."

She laughed. "Ah, it's fine. You've never seen me drinking with Addie. We may be little and cute, but we both can drink anyone under the table."

"Something tells me I should believe that. I'm just worried about you."

"I'm okay. I'm tougher than I look."

"All right. Fine." I sat down across from her. "Is there anything that you can remember from your last mission before our date?"

She shook her head. "It was supposed to be pretty standard. My team was a four-person, one of them Addie, the others were Tomlinson and Grey. Both solid, younger agents. No disciplinary actions on them. They follow orders well. Just standard stuff. The target was a dick and a human trafficker. And while in the process of apprehension, I sort of knifed him to death. But he wasn't a member of Victus. My name isn't on any chatter circles or anything like that."

My brow furrowed at that. "And before that, anything off-kilter that you can remember? When was the last time you went after Victus?"

She frowned, and I could see her mentally riffling through her memory. "I don't know. A year ago? Two?... Two. Yeah, maybe two. A long time to wait for retribution, don't you think?"

"Think about that date night when Stannis showed up. Anything suspicious then?"

"No. I mean, I got chewed out by Roz before I met you. You know, because... murder."

The way she said it, that look on her face, I couldn't help it. I laughed. "Jesus."

"Look, I'm not a sociopath. I do recognize the loss of human life. It's just that he was filth, and he was going to kill the girls, and I just couldn't let him. And I know that Roz wanted us to use him. I know what the protocol is. I'm not an idiot. Conserve life so that we can get information and cut off the head. It's just that I couldn't let him carry on. He fucked with my idea of righteousness and all that shit, so I let my knife do the talking. And if I'm being honest, I would do it again. A hundred percent."

"Okay, you don't have to explain yourself to me."

"Sorry. Sometimes I just get hot. And I just... You know, it gets the better of me because when I joined, I just wanted to do the right thing. Make the world better. Save people's lives. And if I can't do that, if what I'm doing doesn't accomplish that, then why the hell am I doing it?"

"What did Roz say about that?"

"Oh, God, I'm forever catching a lecture. 'We need to be able to utilize these people, Lyra. Think of the bigger picture, Lyra. You have to use your head, Lyra.' Same bullshit. Different day."

"All right. Do you think that she might know something useful about Tyler? Is she worth approaching again?"

"Well, we have a difference of opinion."

"What does that mean?"

"She is currently very protective of your favorite person."

I frowned. "Why is she protective of the twat?"

She rolled her eyes. "You know what, your guess is as good as mine. She doesn't seem to like him, but she acts like I should kiss his ass."

I frowned. "Do he and Roz have history? With Victus?"

"I guess some time ago, he'd been chasing Pierre Como, one of the founding fathers of Victus, before I joined The Firm."

"How old is this guy anyway?"

She smirked at that.

I was glad my jealousy was amusing her.

"Let's see, I was nineteen when I joined. At the time, he was twenty-three. He was sent on some undercover stuff and then transferred to the New York office for a while."

"Okay, New York office makes sense. So he went after Victus. What happened then?"

"I don't know. Pierre Como was killed. His lieutenants were supposed to be taken out too, but something went wrong. And with that going bad, Tyler was reassigned. That was all before my time."

"So The Firm was after Victus, the missions failed, Tyler was reassigned, and then it all settled down to nothing. But what if he didn't fail? What if exactly what was expected to happen, happened?"

I frowned. "What do you mean?"

"Think about it. He was after Victus, but he only killed one of the heads. The second head, which allowed the organization to thrive, lives and flourishes."

I frowned. "So you're saying that Tyler went bad?"

"I'm just throwing out the possibility."

"That would mean all this time he's been working for them. But that doesn't make any sense, because when he was a Valentine op, he wasn't even on any major terrorism cases. I mean, he was, but he wasn't. He couldn't affect that much change, is what I'm saying."

"Think about the women and men he's been assigned to."

She frowned at that. "Actually, yeah. He's been very good undercover. Or at least he was then. After we split, he became a field agent, so he was a Valentine op for maybe three years. He's been a field agent again since last year."

"Do you think Addie can look into it?"

She nodded. "I can ask her."

"All right. So let's say our theory is right. He's working for Victus. They got to him and have him in their pocket. Why come after you? And so suddenly, out of the blue." I frowned, thinking it through. "Maybe he knows the Whitestop weapons deal is going to take place here in LA."

She picked up on my thread of thought. "Obviously, Victus agents showing up on American soil is going to trip off all kinds of sensors, right?"

"Right."

"So, I guess it's all a distraction. If someone comes after me, no one is going to be paying attention to what Victus is *really* doing."

I shook my head. "By coming after you, that in fact did put him on the map. Because they came after you, The Firm started looking a lot closer."

Her brow furrowed. "Yeah, that doesn't link."

"Every theory I run implies some kind of advanced knowledge. And there's no appropriate reason why they'd be coming after you. For what reason? You're also an agent. What would be the purpose of eliminating you?"

She shook her head. "I don't like the idea that it could be random."

I nodded. Me either. I don't believe in coincidences."

She grinned then. "You sound like Roz. She doesn't believe in fate or coincidence. She believes that everything happens as a matter of consequence."

"She sounds a lot like Michael."

"They'd probably get along like a house on fire."

"Maybe. What if we're looking at this the wrong way?"

"What way is that?" she asked.

I shook my head. "What if he's freelancing?"

She blinked. "But for who?"

"What if some other asshole hired the hit?"

"Yeah, I suppose that's possible. But who is in bed with Victus? That doesn't make any sense."

"Not sure. I'd start by taking a look at who wants you dead."

"You really aren't just going to let me die, are you?"

"Like I said, my feelings for you are real, Lyra. So, whether you like it or not, for now, you're stuck with me. I will do my best to keep you safe."

...

Lyra

He *did* care about me.

All this time, I'd been walking around not trusting him, not believing him. But he'd risked his life now two, three times to save me?

That wasn't a man who was just doing his duty. That wasn't a man who just happened to be there and did the right thing. That was a man who loved me.

I lifted my gaze up to his. "Thank you, Marcus."

He lifted a brow. "For what?"

"You saved my life a bunch of times. I feel like being grateful is the least I can do."

"Yeah, well, you're too cute to let die. Especially first thing in the morning when you're extra cranky and haven't had coffee."

"I'm not cranky."

"Yes, you are. Very cranky, but it's cute because you scrunch your nose up when you look like you're about to murder someone."

"Stop. I'm being serious."

He sobered immediately. "You know I would do anything to keep you safe, right?"

I nodded slowly. "Yeah, I'm sorry I'm just seeing that now."

"Well, it's a good thing I'm patient."

I laughed at that. "Marcus?"

His voice dropped to a whisper. "Yes, Lyra?"

"Make love to me?"

The grin that spread over his lips was slow and sexy, tantalizing and seductive. "No scratching your itch this time?"

I shook my head. "I mean, I have all kinds of itches that need to be scratched, but this time, I just want you."

"Understood. And for the record, I've never stopped wanting you. I'm sorry our jobs and who we are got in the way."

I shook my head then. "I don't think it did. Right from the start, we've been paired because we were exactly who we were supposed to be."

And then I wrapped my arms around him. Drawing myself up onto my tiptoes, I brushed my lips softly over his. I could feel the vibration through his body. That low moan that reverberated. I recognized his need instantly because it was exactly what I felt.

"Lyra, you are so beautiful."

I almost didn't hear the whisper because it came out as a low growl just as he was dropping his head back down to mine, kissing me like he wanted to make it count. When our lips met, it was more of a slow sizzle than the scorching inferno of the last couple of times we'd kissed. But that sizzle was no less dangerous, no less combustible. But it also came with trust. *And love*.

Marcus's hands wrapped around my waist, and he pulled me close. So close I could feel every muscle, feel his strength, and there was no hiding the steel bulge pulsing at my belly. "Marcus, it seems like you're happy to see me."

He whispered against my lips. "I'm always happy to see you." Then he lifted me easily, as if I weighed nothing. His hands on my ass gripped me tight, holding me just where I needed him. I groaned against his lips.

He used that opportunity to slide his tongue in, teasing mine, stroking into my mouth, making me want him. Making me need him. Making me see that, all along, this thing between us had been something different. Something special.

Love.

He carried me into the bedroom, and when he laid me on the bed, he didn't waste time, and neither did I as we fought over clothes and how quickly we could shun them. But when we were naked and he crawled over me, he slowed things down. Starting at my toes, he sucked one into his mouth, and I squealed. "Marcus, what are you doing?"

He laughed. "There isn't a spot on you that I don't want to kiss. Even your toes."

When I lifted my head, I saw that he was serious. He kissed the arch of my foot. My ankle. Smoothing his hands up over my calves, he followed that same trail with his lips, his tongue, little nips of his teeth.

When he reached the backside of my knees, I shuddered. I knew where he was going.

He lifted his head. "Oh, you're anticipating now?"

I wanted to say something quippy and funny. But I had nothing. All I could do was moan and nod. "Uh-huh."

He flashed me a wicked grin. Something that made him look younger, more carefree, far less serious. This Marcus was inside him too. The fun one. The playful one. And I couldn't wait to learn about all the parts of him again.

When he reached the apex of my thighs, I thought for sure I was in for another ride like last night. But instead, he gave me one soft kiss on the clit, making my hips buck and rise up off the couch, and then he kept moving. Up to my hips. And then up my belly. When he got to my breasts, he kissed each nipple tenderly but with tongue. Like a soft French kiss. My breath caught, and I whispered, "Marcus, please."

"Oh. We're not done kissing yet. You have to turn over now so I can kiss your back."

I laughed. "You can't be serious."

"Oh, I'm serious."

I shuddered as he rolled me over. He was being thorough. Gently, he moved my hair aside and kissed the nape of my neck. Down along my spine. My shoulder blades. When he reached the dimples just above my ass, he kissed each of them with intention, making me squirm. "Marcus, you're teasing me."

"Yes. As a matter of fact, I am. Just so you get a taste of your own medicine."

"I'm not a tease."

"Oh, Lyra Wilkinson, you are, in fact, a tease. Every smile, every swish of your hips. All of it. You're a tease. Now, I like it, obviously. But you're attempting to torture me, and I've noticed."

I giggled, and he continued his kissing, taking nips at my ass. "Jesus Christ, every part of you is so goddamn gorgeous. It's like a smorgasbord and I don't know where to start."

His lips traveled over the backs of my thighs and returned to the backs of my knees, making me giggle and catch my breath all in the same stroke of his tongue.

By the time he flipped me back over, I was all nerves and sensation and desperate need. I tried pressing my thighs together to help quell the sensations, but he stopped me, separating my thighs easily with his big hands. "Now, now. We talked about this. You're not closing off your pussy to me. I want to see it."

"Marcus, please. God, please."

"I still want to see it."

When I thought he was going to settle in for the torture again, he proved me wrong. Instead, he gave me one of those firm presses against my clit, and then kissed his way back up my torso. Kissing my breasts the same way and then settling on my lips. "Hello, darling."

I watched his eyes. They were full of heat and something else. *Tenderness*.

I could feel the length of him nudge my sex, and I lifted my hips, trying to tempt him. Then he moaned. "I made a rookie mistake. I didn't grab a condom before I started this."

I laughed.

"Stay right here. I'll be right back."

When he started to move, I held onto him tight. "No. We don't need it."

His brows lifted. "Lyra?"

I raised my hips, gyrating over his erection, and he hissed. "You're taunting me."

"I'm not. We have yearly check-ups, and obviously I haven't been with anyone in a while and it's just been you. And I'm on birth control."

He swallowed hard then. "It's just… Are you sure you want that?"

I encased his beautiful face in my hands, stroking over his stubble and tracing his lips with my thumb. "Yeah. I want everything."

His eyes searched mine, looking for uncertainty. But he must have seen the truth. That all I wanted was him.

He didn't even need to line us up. We were a perfect match.

He drew his hips back, watching me. And then he notched his hips forward. The smooth tip of his erection entered, stretching me, and I held my breath.

"Lyra, are you sure?"

I nodded vehemently and lifted my gaze to meet his. "Yeah. Make me yours for real."

When he notched forward even further, I blew out a breath. "Oh, fuck. This feels so good. I haven't... ever... oh God."

He drew back slightly, and I complained, trying to claw him back. "Woman, you're trying to kill me. I'm attempting to have some control here."

Sweat had popped on his brow. His teeth grazed his bottom lip as he notched forward again, this time, sliding all the way home. The curse on his lips made me want to chuckle. His little, "Fuck me," said in his British accent and followed by a string of British curses I wasn't sure I understood, made me realize that he was fighting for control too. Just like I was.

We stayed like that for seconds, minutes, hours, I don't know. And then he started to move, his control back under a tight leash. Rocking. Notching his hips. Faster, faster. Then getting bolder as his hands flipped between us to crush my breasts. And then he put his hand to either side of me and pushed up, bracing himself above me and watching as he made love to me. He whispered murmurs of, "Oh God. You feel so good. You're so beautiful," were all I needed to hear. Both of us, with our bruised and slightly battered bodies, were ignoring any pain we might have felt and giving in to the sensation.

I could tell when his control snapped against the leash though. Marcus changed our position and sat up. Notched my legs wider with his hands. Gripping my hips as he brought me to him over and over again. His teeth clenched. The muscle in his jaw was pulsing. Sweat was dripping off his brow, and all I could do was hold on to the headboard and lift my hips when commanded.

He meant business. And his business was my pleasure, because that orgasm was coming to me whether I was ready for it or not. The way he watched me with intensity, I would never get over that. That subtle claim that this was us, together. I was his, and he was mine. As my toes started to go numb with all the blood rushing to the apex of my thighs, I arched my back, placing my hands flat on the headboard and pushing against him. Taking him even deeper. His growl was feral as he leaned forward and claimed one of my breasts with his mouth, sucking deep. One hand on my ass, the other reaching between us and giving me hard, firm strokes over my clit. I choked out a cry. "Oh my God. Marcus."

Around my nipple, he growled, "Let go."

And I had no choice, really, with that accent, the low command. Who knew I was down with being bossed around in bed?

The orgasm slammed into me, making me moan and quiver. There was no getting around it. Marcus Black knew his way around my body. Knew how to get exactly the response he wanted. Knew what I needed. Even as pure bliss pulsed through me and everything from my toes to my fingertips twitched and pulsed, he didn't let up. He just gave me a wicked grin and kept going.

When I started begging, he slowed. "Oh, my darling wants a break?"

I nodded. "I can't take anymore."

"Oh, I think you can."

But still, he pulled out. And I missed him immediately. That stretch, the fullness of him.

But it seemed Marcus wasn't done with me. He turned me over, grabbed a pillow, and placed it under my hips and lower abdomen, tilting me just so. Then he moved back into place with one smooth stroke, and I shouted, "Oh my God."

His chuckle was feral as he leaned over and nipped at the base of my neck. "God, I'm so deep now. Can you feel that?"

I whimpered. "Yes. Oh my God, please don't stop."

And he didn't. The nips continued. And when he pulled back, both hands on my ass, all I could do was press against the headboard again, hoping to keep myself level at some point. But he did all the work. Rotating his hips, slamming forward. Keeping me hovering on the edge. And then he reached under me, lifting my hips again just so. All while pumping. His fingers found my clit. This time, the stroking was gentle. Easy. Lazy almost as he worked his hips. His whisper was low. "Oh, there's my love. Nice and easy for you. How do you like that?"

"Marcus, it's so good. So, so good."

"Good. This *should* feel good. I have a surprise for you too." When his thumb grazed over the pucker of my ass, there was no stopping it. The quick flash of electric fire. And then I was coming. Somewhere from the deep depth of my soul, I let out a roar as he gently stroked my pucker. Fingers on my clit as he made love to me. And then I could feel him, almost as if he grew bigger, stretched me wider. And then his words came tumbling out of his mouth. "Bugger. Fuck me. Jesus Christ."

Then I could feel him finally letting go. Losing all control as he tumbled over the edge with me.

12

LYRA

A thumb rolling over my nipple was what woke me. "Oh my God, again? How are you not tired?"

Marcus's chuckle was a low rumble. "Have you seen yourself? That's enough to keep me up most nights."

I grinned. "Or several times a night."

When I'd gone to him last night and asked him to make love to me, he'd wasted no time.

And I was glad I'd stopped hesitating. He wasn't Tyler. He wouldn't hurt me like that. With Marcus, I wouldn't be left with that shamed, embarrassed feeling, like I'd done wrong somehow. I knew I would miss him, and losing him would break me, most definitely. But until that happened, I would enjoy my time with him at the very least.

When he kissed into my hair, I moaned again. "Ugh, I need a shower. And please tell me we've got decent food in the cabinets."

"You're in luck. Since Rhodes stocked the place, we should be good. He likes the finer things in life, you know. He's into caviar and those kinds of things."

I wrinkled my nose at the mention of caviar. "I need real

food. Eggs. Bacon. Oh my God, tell me there is bacon and stuff for pancakes."

He laughed and rolled me over on my back. Between my thighs, I could feel the length of him growing, and I said, "You were serious?"

He nodded and dipped his head to gently give me a kiss. "Yeah, I was dead serious."

And then he lifted his head, met my gaze, and slid in again. "Ahhh." He groaned, and I moaned. Then I lifted my hips to meet his. This time there was no foreplay, no teasing, just the two of us, fingers intertwined, both trying to race to the finish line. And just when I was there, he tore his lips from mine, dragging them across my cheek and down to my neck as he growled, "God, you're so fucking sexy. I missed you."

All I could mutter was, "I missed you too," followed by, "oh my God, oh my God." And then his hand reached between us and his thumb gently stroked my clit. He pulled his head back to watch me. With his other big hand, he clamped mine together up over my head, and all I could do was submit to the torture. That sweet, exquisite torture. My hips rose, again and again. "Oh my God, Marcus. Marcus, Jesus." And then I broke apart around the thick length of him as he held perfectly still.

"Ah, there's my girl."

And then he was pulled out.

"Where the fuck are you going?"

His grin and chuckle had me laughing. He rolled me over onto my stomach and then pulled my hips up before tapping my ass with a sharp crack. "Shit," I gasped. "Marcus."

"Oh God, that's pretty." And then he slammed home. All I could do was bury my head in the pillow and scream as another orgasm ripped through me.

When one of his thumbs grazed over the pucker of my ass, I stopped breathing. And as he gently pushed, I coughed and then began begging. "Oh God, please. Please, right there. Please more. Please. Please, please. Just please."

When his arm tightened around my waist, my back flush up against his chest, his body went stiff as his teeth grazed my shoulder with enough pressure to leave a love bite. He'd marked me. I was his. Forever.

Not a bad place to be. He eased me gently on the bed before rolling us both to the side with him still inside me. "Oh my God, you're going to kill me," he gasped.

"Me? I was just laying here. Minding my business."

"Yeah, but then your arse was calling out to me. You see, this is really your arse's fault."

I giggled, and my laugh almost drowned out the scream from the other room.

We both froze. And without even having to say anything, he eased out of me, and we both rolled out of bed. He tossed a T-shirt and a pair of boxers at me as he pulled on the same.

And then we both grabbed our guns and silencers and tiptoed to the living room. It was still dark outside.

The clock in the kitchen read four-thirty, which meant dawn was coming soon.

So who the fuck was there?

Before I knew what was happening, there were agents rushing inside the safe house. Too many of them.

And without having to exchange any words, Marcus and I put our backs to each other, and faced the assailants.

It was all happening in slow motion, like in a movie.

They clearly wanted it quiet because the assassins they'd sent had knives instead of guns. Knives were messy and bloody. But we were in a little house out in the suburbs. No one might come looking for us for days until the house manager came back to clean.

A guy, just a little taller than me, came toward me with a knife between his index and middle finger.

He said nothing, but he came at me quick. I popped off two rounds and turned to get the one by the door too. He managed to release one of his knives though, and I shoved Marcus just out of the way as it whizzed by his chest.

He gasped. "Jesus, fuck."

We didn't have time to talk though. The next assailant came at me. I fired and missed as he cut a slice with the knife down the outer part of my arm. When I hissed, Marcus shouted over his shoulder, "You good?"

"Yep, let me kill this guy real quick."

The second shot didn't miss, but I was cognizant of how many bullets I had left.

The next guy wasn't a guy at all but a woman. Slight stature, slightly shorter than me, but Jesus Christ, she was fast. She moved her body like a tiny demon. We fought then. Hand to hand. Every block I tried, she knew it better. Every angle I turned, she delivered kicks.

I was too busy covering my own ass to even worry about Marcus. All I heard were oofs and aahs and grunts, but I had to trust he was okay because if I took my eye off the ball, that slice down the arm would be the least of my worries. Even though it hurt like a son of a bitch.

As she aimed a punch for my face, I was able to slide and deflect it with my left arm, hooking her right wrist with my hand, locking my hand around it, then tucking my left arm up under her. Using her momentum against her, I flipped her over and slammed her down onto her back. Still controlling her arm, I delivered a series of left jabs to her face. She tried to fight back, but then I planted a knee on her arm and continued to deliver blows until she stopped moving.

I picked my gun up off the floor when I saw an assailant heading for Marcus's back.

I shot him. And then I noticed another shadow coming in

the window, but instead of going for me or Marcus, it went for one of the two assailants Marcus was fighting with.

I wanted to shoot one of them, but I couldn't be sure I wasn't going to hit Marcus.

Even as I rose, one of the other guys Marcus had taken down was crawling across the floor, trying to reach for a gun. I aimed my gun at him, but all I heard was a *click, click*. Out of bullets. Goddamn it.

I was forced to launch myself and roll with him, wrestling for control of the gun.

When he rolled on top of me, his arms were strong enough to wrap around my neck, and my vision started to go gray.

Fuck. Not a good look. Rookie move. Absolutely the worst position for a woman to be in. Forcing my brain to quiet, I tried to remember my training, letting my muscles do what they wanted. What they'd been trained to do.

I made my hands into C's, then in one swift motion, brought them down with all the force I could muster along the edge of his thumbs, forcing his hands off my neck. Then, dragging in a gulp of air, I did what was the hardest/simplest part, brought my elbows to my knees.

That momentum sent him flying over my head and landing on his back. Then I took control of his arm, wrapped my leg over his head, and arm-barred him. Just leaning my body back, and praying that I was strong enough, had a good enough hold to render him lifeless. Finally, he stopped moving, dropped the gun, and then I rolled, picked it up, turned, and shot.

When I turned back to the fray, that's when I saw little red dots.

"Marcus, down!"

He didn't even flinch. He followed my direction immediately. The snipers took out the guy he was fighting and the one who was fighting the secondary man who had entered through the window. That left one assailant still standing. With the gun I had in my palm, I aimed, fired, and he went down.

Marcus's voice was loud but stern. "Okay?"

"Yep, I'm fine. Just bleeding from the arm, but other than that, I'm good."

Then groaning came from one of the bodies on the floor. The guy who had been helping Marcus. We both crawled over to him and peeled off his mask. I was surprised to find a familiar face. "Tyler? What the fuck?"

He gasped. "Fuck. Fuck. Fuck."

"Start talking."

Marcus rolled him over slightly to check his injury. "He's hit. Chest wound. I don't have what it takes to fix that."

Tyler thrashed on the ground. "I'm done. I won't make it."

"Tyler, what the fuck is going on?"

Tyler grabbed for me and I took his hand. "You need to be careful... Roz."

I frowned at him. "What the fuck are you talking about?"

"Roz... She did this."

"No, there's no way. She loves me."

He pulled me closer. His voice was weaker, but still carried the deep timbre I was more than familiar with. "I loved you, too. I did." A cold shiver ran through me, and I tried to pull away, but he held on tight. "She told me... She made me dump you."

My brow furrowed, and I shook my head. "No, she wouldn't. She loves me. She's my mentor. She trained me."

"Roz... your father... affair. He chose your mother."

The words he was saying were bouncing off me like my body and brain had formed a shield around me for protection. "No, I-I don't understand."

"You saw something you shouldn't have. She sent Prochenko to kill you. She called me in to make sure. She thinks I work for her... but... been protecting you." He jerkily reached for his pocket and pulled out a flash drive. "Proof is here."

I stared down at it. "What? No, Tyler... I don't understand. What do you know about my father?" But he wasn't moving anymore, and his hand fell from mine, no longer holding tight.

Marcus was pulling me away from Tyler. When did he get a bag? "What? When did you pack that?"

"I always have a go-bag. Come on, we need to get out of here."

But I held on to Tyler. "No, wake up, Tyler. Please tell me everything."

Marcus wrapped his arm around my waist and pulled me from the floor. And then he was shoving shoes onto my feet. "We have to go right now."

I had no choice. I had to leave Tyler there, bleeding out on the floor. He was already gone.

LYRA

After what had happened to Tyler, Marcus thought it was safest to hide in plain sight.

The Four Seasons was the best place to be for a meetup.

It had been some time since I'd been there. The last time was for a job. Mostly surveillance at a party, so I hadn't really fully enjoyed it before. But now we strolled into the bar in the far corner of the lobby to meet Rhodes. "You two look well for a pair of deceased agents."

Marcus growled at him. "Not funny."

Rhodes winced. "Sorry, you lost your friend," he said while looking at me with concern in his eyes.

"He wasn't a friend. He was—"

Marcus sighed. "It's complicated."

"How did they know you were there?"

I shook my head. "I don't know."

Marcus and Rhodes exchanged glances. "Maybe the clothes Addie packed for you were tracked."

"The dresses were mine. Addie just brought them for me, Marcus."

"Well, you were being tracked somehow," Rhodes said.

"You also have a sat phone, Lyra, and again, Addie gave that to you." He glanced away as if he hated suggesting that possibility to me.

I reached into the crossbody bag I had and slid the sat phone across the table to Rhodes. "Check it."

"I will. But there she is. You can ask her yourself."

Addie didn't look like Addie. She had on a dark wig, and the hair was pulled up in a ponytail. She even had little tendrils flowing down on her face. Not just in a bullshit way with bangs to hide the lines. This one looked real. She had cat-eye glasses on as well. And her outfit was very librarian chic.

"Someone has been shopping."

She grinned at me then. "Well, you said to come incognito, so I've been all over LA, trying to shake the initial tail that I had. When I did, I had to change clothes in a boutique. The wig was my own. I had it in the car."

Marcus frowned. "Funny you should mention a tail, because someone has been tracking our girl Lyra here."

Addie's brow lifted. "And you think it's me?"

"Who else? We switched to two different safe houses. And twice now, she almost died in front of me. I'm not taking any more chances. That's why Rhodes is going to take you in there," he pointed at the restrooms down the hall, "and he's going to scan you for trackers."

Addie shook her head. "If you think for one minute—"

Rhodes grinned at her. "Now, I've got a soft touch, and we're in a very public place, so you'll be safe with me. What with all the people swarming around, not to mention the cameras everywhere, even the dumbest douche wouldn't do anything criminal in this place. So let's go ahead and do this all nice and civilized, yeah?"

She glowered at me then. "You really think I would do this to you, Lyra?"

"Of course not, Addie, but if you were me—"

"Yes, I'd be suspicious too. But I also know that you love me, so I'm doing this for your sake."

My lips twitched. She got it, all right. She was just putting on a show for Marcus and Rhodes, who stood and gestured toward the restroom gallantly as he asked, "Shall we?"

She growled at Rhodes, and he grinned at her.

I could see it, there was a spark there. But I didn't want to look at it too closely. She sauntered toward the restroom, and he followed her. I knew for a fact the bathroom at the end of the hall was unisex, and I hoped that the search for a tracker didn't get too intimate.

"Oh boy, Addie is going to eat him alive."

I turned to Marcus then. "So I'm not the only one seeing sparks between them?"

He shook his head. "No, you're not the only one seeing that. The two of them are like a combustion engine, waiting to blow up. I'm not sure that's a good thing."

"I have to agree."

"All right, so if it's not Addie, then how are you being tracked? There has to be another way."

"I mean, Addie brought weapons, but they wouldn't have been from the Firm's armory. We have to sign all those in and out. We all have our own private stash. So unless one of my weapons was—" I frowned.

"What is it?"

I shook my head. "I'm not sure. But I mean, it had to be my weapons or shoes. I wasn't wearing any of the clothes that Addie brought me."

"Okay, a weapon, or something. Earrings, a necklace, a watch?"

"I don't keep any of those on me."

Addie and Rhodes returned, and Addie plopped into the seat next to me. "See, my darling? I'm clean. Your friend Rhodes here was very thorough."

I winced. "Ads."

"Oh, relax. He just ran over me with one little thingy. I'm clean. I'm not being tracked. The question is, how are *you* being tracked, Lyra? The clothes I brought you are brand new from the store. Including the La Perla."

I flushed thinking about the panties that she'd picked out for me. "Thanks for that, Ads."

Rhodes winked at me. "Well, congratulations Marcus."

Marcus just smirked. He was some help.

"All right then, think. If there's a way that I'm being tracked, we'll have to figure it out. Because twice now, we've almost died. And after what Tyler said, I can't let it go. I have to pull the thread."

She frowned. "Since when are we listening to Tyler?"

Marcus, Rhodes, and I exchanged glances. Then I filled Addie in on what had happened. Slowly I watched as she processed the information. "You're fucking kidding me."

I shook my head. "I'm not. That's why we're here and not somewhere more secure. We're also meeting here because there are no less than four exits, and it's probably better if neither one of you knows our room number."

She sighed. "Fucking hell. Goddamn Tyler. Why did he have to turn out to be a hero?"

"I think *hero* is a bit of an overstatement. But he did come to save my ass, so I'm grateful."

"Wait a minute," Addie said. "So this whole time... Roz *made* him break up with you?"

I swallowed that pain again. I'd spent the last two years of my life hating Tyler. Absolutely loathing him. I had cried on Roz's shoulder. I could still remember how she'd told me that it was for the best. She had lied to my face. She'd hurt me, and then she'd lied about it.

Marcus slid a hand over my knee and squeezed gently, and I forced myself to drive my attention back to the conversation. "Yeah."

"But Roz loves you. *Actually* loves you. She's like your mother."

"Let's operate under the idea that there's no such thing as love at The Firm. Then what would you say?"

Addie blinked. "Well, okay, a little insulted, but yeah, I'll go with it. So then all these years she's been manipulating you? And what's this about your dad?"

"Yeah, that's what I need you to help me with. See if you can figure out what the hell Tyler was talking about, because none of that makes sense."

Rhodes nodded. "I'll have a look on our side, too. I have the clearance." He focused on Marcus. "But honestly, bro, it's time to loop Michael and Maggie in on the truth."

He sighed at that. "Yeah fine. You're probably right. But they're not going to just accept it at face value. That means you'll have to come in, Lyra. Would you do that?"

"I can't believe any of this is happening."

"Look, Tyler has thrown us some kind of tip. So we just have to figure out what the fuck is going on exactly. Whatever it is, it isn't what we expected. But if he's right, then you saw something you weren't supposed to see. Which means we have to figure out what it was and how to use it to save your life."

LYRA

"You want to do what?"

"I'm going to talk to her." I said, my voice sounding hollow to my own ears.

Addie just sat with her elbows on her knees and her hands covering her face. "That's not a good idea, Lyra."

"What else am I supposed to do? I can still feel Tyler's blood sticking between my fingers."

Marcus rubbed his hands up and down my back, trying to soothe me. I knew what he was doing, and I welcomed it, but right then I wanted to feel the rage. I wanted to feel the fire.

Rhodes was busy decrypting the flash drive that Tyler had slipped to me. He was quiet, but every time I spoke, I could see him visibly wincing. Probably too much emotion for him. Finally, he sat back. "I'm not saying that you should or you shouldn't confront Roz, but I am saying I have information for you."

I stood immediately, and Marcus took my hand. "Let's have a look."

Rhodes slid his computer where everyone could see it, and even Addie strained to look, though I could tell she was despondent. Addie was all about The Firm, even more so than me. She'd come in young. So young they'd recruited her from juvie, despite that sweet face.

Her stepfather had been a piece of shit who abused her, and when she told her mother, she refused to believe Addie's accusations. So Addie had to deal with the problem herself. She had nearly made him a eunuch. Unfortunately, he lived, and she got sent to juvie. But that was where she'd been found by The Firm, thanks to her penchant for getting into trouble and breaking into files. The warden at the juvenile detention center where she'd been sentenced would have sworn Addie had broken out more than once but could never prove it because she'd always come back.

I once asked her why she'd gone back, and she said it was because she had nowhere else to go. The Firm had given her a new life. So I could see how she didn't want to rock that boat, but she was still there with me, wasn't she?

Rhodes made a couple of quick taps and pulled up everything I needed to know on the screen. I studied the photos and documents closely, not fully understanding what I was seeing at first.

"I don't understand?"

"Mostly these are agent files. Histories, blind spots, et cetera."

I noticed a couple of files he'd highlighted, Agents Rogue and Renegade. They were firm agents for around ten years. Renegade was high-level, and Rogue was not too far behind him.

I shook my head. "Who are these people? Why do they matter?"

Marcus said, "Renegade became a trainer for incoming agents. He trained Rogue."

I blinked in surprise. "Jesus. Can we talk to him?"

He sighed. "No, we can't speak to him. He's dead."

I cursed under my breath. "Fuck. He would have certainly been someone to give us some insight. What about Rogue?"

Rhodes glanced around, and Marcus frowned at him. "Mate, what is it?"

He sighed. "She was killed in a car accident with her husband… Renegade."

Icicles formed in my belly, and then those icicles had little baby tendrils that formed even smaller icicles. I shook my head. "No."

Rhodes continued. "Lyra, I'm sorry, but your parents were both Firm agents."

I shook my head. "Nope, no, I don't believe you."

"Believe what you want. But the files that your friend Tyler died giving to you show they weren't who you thought they were."

I shook my head again. "No, no, it's not possible."

Addie reached for me, but I darted out of her grip. "No, I don't need soothing. This isn't right. My mother was on the PTA. She gardened. She was into fashion design. My father mowed the lawn all the time. He worked a lot, but God, he wasn't an agent. He was an engineer."

Marcus examined the screen. "Yes, it says that he was one of The Firm's best hackers before he became a trainer. And your mother was an outstanding field agent."

Bile rose up in my throat, and tears stung my eyes. Then I felt Marcus grip me around my waist, and his chin tucked into my hair. "Shhh. It's okay. Hush, love. Just process the information. Knowing this changes nothing about who they were to you. Your mother was on the PTA. Great. She gardened, absolutely. She made pretty things. She was also an agent. She could be both."

"But they never said anything to me."

Addie's voice was soft. "They probably didn't want you in this life. Because think of everything we've done in the last year alone."

I was going to be sick. "They were killed. So it wasn't a car accident?"

Rhodes, who I was starting to quite dislike by now, muttered, "It was a car, but it wasn't an accident. It was a car bomb."

"Jesus. Did someone accept responsibility?" I asked.

They all exchanged glances, and Addie said, "It doesn't say."

I turned in his arms and stared at Marcus as he said, "This changes nothing. Right now the focus is on saving your life. You can learn more about your parents and who they were after we know you're safe. Do you understand me?"

I nodded. He was right. I didn't have a choice. I had to focus on the task at hand, which was not dying.

"Roz kept this from me."

Addie's voice had sting in it. "Fuck her bullshit. All these years, even I've seen it. She's made it seem like she was your mother figure. That you had no one else. That your life started when you joined The Firm. She manipulated you."

Seeing it through Addie's eyes as it peeled away a layer of what The Firm meant to her made me feel less alone. Her brow had dropped into a deep furrow. "She lied to you."

She had, in fact, lied to me. The woman who was my mentor. My friend. She made me into something my parents likely hadn't wanted for me. I had become that boogeyman. And it made me sick.

"Tyler. She sent him to spy on me, but instead he tried to save my life."

Marcus nodded and then kissed me on the forehead. "She separated the two of you. How do you feel about that?"

"Honestly, I don't know. I spent a lot of energy hating him because I thought he'd lied to me. But he was trying to protect me all along, and I trusted the wrong person." She'd separated us on purpose because we were too close.

Marcus's hands on my hips tightened. "It's okay, Lyra. It happens. Whatever the play is, we'll do that. I don't want you to get hurt."

I lifted my head and met his gaze. "I don't have a choice. She's not going to give me any answers. She orchestrated this, sent people to kill me. Sent *Tyler* to kill me. So yeah, we're going to take her down."

Addie just nodded. "Right. We're going to need weapons. Lots and lots of weapons. Good thing I know a guy."

I glanced over at her and gave her a nod of thanks. She only shrugged. "She lied to both of us, Lyra. But you had a shot, a real chance of not being in this mess. And she ruined it, on purpose, so she could control you. And that's just fucked. I never had a chance, but you know I hate liars and manipulators. So let's go blow some shit up."

I blinked away watery tears as I smiled at her. "I love you."

"I love you more."

This was dangerous. There was no way I wanted any of these three involved, but I knew I needed help. Besides, there was no way any of them, even Rhodes, was going to let me do this on my own.

13

LYRA

"You don't have to do this," I said as the men were loading themselves up with weapons.

Addie raised her arms and let the bulletproof vest slide over her body. It looked like very thin chain mail. Or like a sparkly top she was going to wear at a club. But then she put Kevlar over it. "Look, where you go, I go. I thought that would be apparent by now."

"Yeah, but where I go feels crazy."

"Maybe, but just because it's crazy doesn't mean it's wrong."

"Roz lied to me," I said again.

Addie nodded. "Yeah, she did."

"And what's this bullshit about my parents? Jesus, Addie, she lied to me about them too."

"I know, love."

I shook my head. "This was less about Tyler and more about who I was when my parents died, what I needed, how hurt I'd been. She was the one to orchestrate it all, and all this time, she just lied to my face."

"Yeah, she did. The question is, what are you going to do

about it? Because right now, we're putting on this tech gear which means we're anticipating getting shot at by the woman who lied to you, the woman who possibly sent people to kill you. For that alone, I'd prefer to just walk in there and shoot her. You, on the other hand, want to have a conversation. It's your call, so you just tell me how you want this to go, and that's how it will go."

"What did I do to deserve you?"

"You mean a generally awesome bestie, who's going to make sure that Roz pays for everything she's done?"

"Yeah. I must have been excellent in another life. Besides, all her bullshit about doing the right thing, and she's got people at Victus on her payroll."

Addie nodded. "I can deal with a lot. But not someone who works with terrorists. I mean, that's just a line."

I laughed at that. "I love you, Addie."

"What is all this love nonsense? Don't go getting mushy on me."

"Right, yeah. Never mushy."

"We're about to go kick ass. While this soft, gooey Lyra is very cute, and I'm sure Mr. Hot and Handsome over there likes her very much, I need badass Lyra right now. You know, the one who *accidentally*," she said using air quotes, "kills human traffickers. Where is she? Because that's who we need."

I rolled my eyes. "I killed one guy."

"Ah, to be fair, you have killed more than one guy."

"You know what I mean."

She laughed. "And let's face it, you would kill him again."

"Right, because he needed killing."

"Uh-huh."

I rolled my eyes. "What do I want out of this whole situation? Answers. Turns out I don't know who she is, or who the hell *I* am, or why she's been in my life this whole time. And that bullshit she pulled with Tyler? I want to know why."

"Okay, now that I know the objective, I can shoot her to hell."

I blinked in surprise. "What?"

"Lyra, you don't owe her anything. She doesn't deserve your time. You haven't done anything wrong. And I know that's what is eating at you. Where did you go wrong? Why didn't you see this? But this isn't on you. This is on her."

I nodded. "Yeah. I hear you."

"I know you hear me, but listen, okay? We're going to go in there, find out what's going on, find out who she sent to kill you and why, and put a stop to it. And then I'm going to put a bullet in her head."

"A little violent, don't you think?"

"Fine, I will call the police and send her to jail. Are you happy?"

Marcus came back then. "No one's putting a bullet in anyone's head today. When I send her to a black site and let her get tortured for a while, *then* I'll put a bullet in her head."

Rhodes strolled up then. "None of you are very imaginative. There are a million and one ways to torture people. As a matter of fact, you could—"

Marcus shook his head. "Nope, you can't. No one wants to hear it."

"What? Now you're squeamish?" Rhodes asked.

"Yeah. No one wants to hear that."

Addie grinned. "Well, I kind of want to hear it."

I rolled my eyes. "No one's putting a bullet in anyone's head. No one's torturing anyone either. I want answers. That's all. And then we're going to have her arrested." I straightened my shoulders as I strapped in the extra clips for my gun. "Besides, I want her torture to last. And her sitting in prison with the very same people she helped to put there over the years seems like a special kind of torture to me."

"So what are we doing, *exactly*, then?" Addie asked.

Marcus took over, outlining the plan. "Well, you want quick and easy. Walk-in, take out any opposition, capture and retrieve. We're not shooting anyone."

I grinned at Marcus. "Not yet."

He laughed. "That's it. That's all there is. And then we return to the safe house. We'll only have a couple of hours before Firm agents will be all over us. This isn't exactly a sanctioned op, so we just have the four of us. The key is to stay together. No cowboy bullshit." Marcus glanced at Rhodes when he said that.

His friend shook his head. "Mate, don't say that in front of the women. We can't have them thinking I'm unreliable."

Marcus just rolled his eyes. "You're reliable. You'll get the job done. You just might nearly get everyone killed in the process."

He shrugged. "What's life without a little spice?"

Addie just laughed. "Oh my God, that's a party I can get behind."

Marcus took my face in his hands. "Are you sure you want to do this? We can run. I'll protect you. Get a new cover ID, the works. Please choose that option."

I shook my head. "No. I'm not choosing that option. I'm fighting for my life here. I want answers, and this is the only way to get them."

He nodded. "Okay, let's go. I'll follow your lead."

LYRA

MAYBE, just maybe, there was a small part of me that thought this would be easy.

Just stroll up to Roz's house and walk in like nothing was amiss. But this was Roz, and nothing about her would ever be easy. I wore an unassuming black shirt, black pants and black jacket. The color black generally did nothing for me, but it blended into the background, and when you were a spy, that was what you wanted. And unlike the rest of my team, I was walking in through the front fucking door.

I had been there enough times to know the security perimeters fairly well. After all, for most holidays, hadn't this always been the home that I'd been pulled into? Since my parents were gone, Roz had taken over, hadn't she?

My brain still couldn't accept that it was all a lie, that none of it was real. That she had singlehandedly sought to destroy my life, even before I knew her.

All I wanted was some fucking answers. And she'd better have them for me.

Or what? Are you going to kill her? Is that really you, Lyra?

It wasn't me. But honestly, at that point I didn't even know what I was capable of. I had so much anger stored up I didn't know what to do with it all.

I had to see this through. I could still feel the warm stickiness of Tyler's blood on my hands, could still hear his parting words. *Roz did this.* And there was just no way I could forget that. No way I could accept it.

I swallowed hard and rang the doorbell.

When she opened the door, she smiled at me. "Is there a reason you've been standing there for the last five minutes?"

"Oh, you know, I was... daydreaming."

"Well, come on in. I have to say I'm surprised to see you. Aren't you supposed to be on vacation? I figured I wouldn't hear from you for at least a couple more days. I'd thought you'd be on the beach somewhere soaking up some sun."

I stuck out my arms. "I think I've got enough sun, don't you?"

She laughed. "Oh, Lyra, you're so funny. Come on in. Make yourself comfortable."

I could smell onions and garlic wafting from the kitchen. "Oh, I didn't mean to interrupt your dinner."

She laughed. "Lyra, when have you ever interrupted me? You saved me from a night of briefing recruits. Come on and join me."

Roz's house was all chrome and glass on the interior. It was the kind of decor from Hollywood movies. But instead of being cold, it was warm and inviting because of the pops of color she used everywhere and the vivid paintings on the walls. I recognized several Xander Chase photos.

I followed her inside and said, "Thanks."

"Are you sure I can't make you a plate?"

"Yeah, I'm sure. I don't want to take up too much of your time. I just want to talk to you for a bit."

I glanced around to be sure she was alone. This should be easy. Still, my stomach flipped and flopped. My body was telling me I did not want to do this thing.

She sighed as she jogged the rest of the way to the stove. She turned down the burner that was lit and stirred the contents before pulling up her wooden spoon to swipe her index finger over it and sample a taste. "Sure you don't want to try this sauce? I can tell you how I tortured an Italian mobster for it."

I blinked at her. "What?"

"The sauce. It was his mama's secret family recipe."

I shook my head. "There's no way you tortured someone for a sauce recipe."

"Oh, I did. It was a parting gift."

"What?"

She laughed. "Oh relax, Lyra, it's just a joke." But something about the way she said it and the flatness of her eyes told me that it was no joke. At the same time, a cold sensation of warning slid up my neck, telling me it was not safe there.

Listen to your gut. Not safe. Get out.

But I knew Marcus, Rhodes, and Addie were already breaking in. There was no backing out now. She grabbed two wine glasses and handed them to me. Then she reached into the wine fridge and pulled out a bottle of red. "We'll let the sauce sit for a few minutes and have a glass of wine, and then we'll eat."

"Roz, I didn't come for dinner."

"I know, I know. But you're here, so you might as well eat, right?"

"You sound like an over-protective mother."

"And in so many ways I am, aren't I?"

I let her pour the glasses, even though I didn't trust them. She might seem like that mentor-mother type that I had been clinging to since I was nineteen, but this woman had me followed and nearly killed. She should never ever be underestimated.

"Can we talk now? Like talk, talk? I have something important to ask you."

"Yes, Lyra, we can talk. But honestly, wouldn't you rather just have a nice night and enjoy a glass of wine first?"

I shook my head.

"Fine, be that way, but I'm going to have a glass."

I ignored her attempt to deviate from the inevitable. "This is about Tyler."

"Look, I know you're here to complain about something he's done, right? Why don't you just fuck him again and have it done with? At least then I can stop worrying about the two of you. Fucking just has a way of getting out all the cobwebs, doesn't it? So Lyra, love, what is it you have to say about Tyler this time?"

"He told me something interesting."

"Yes, get on with it, darling, before you make me feel bad about drinking by myself."

"Tyler said that *you* separated us."

Her glass slowed on the way to her lips. "Wow." She blinked at me. "I never thought he'd tell you."

All I could do was stare at her. Because even though I knew the truth, even though I'd seen the bug she'd planted on me and understood that Tyler was right, that he had told me the truth as he lay dying in my arms, I still couldn't believe that she had done this to me.

"Yes, I did separate you." She took a sip of her wine. "It was really for the best. You were getting too attached. He was getting distracted. While Control wants you to date, they don't want you to form actual emotional attachments. That would be dangerous. You were young and naive and didn't know any better."

"Wow, so it's true then."

"Of course, it's true darling. You are my best creation. I wasn't going to let him endanger that."

"Your *creation*?"

She sighed. "You know what your problem is, Lyra? You're always so literal. Sometimes training you is just exhausting. Yes, you're my creation. I created you. Before I recruited you, what were you? Sad and lonely and desperate, missing your mommy and daddy." She rolled her eyes.

I'd never seen it before then. The malice under her every word, her every action. This woman whom I had loved almost as much as my own mother, she'd never been benevolent. She had never loved me. All of this was some sick game of what, control?

"So, you created me, did you?"

"Yes, my darling. Everything you are is a result of my training. My tutelage. Even now as you're sitting in front of me questioning my decisions about Tyler, there's a part of you that sees things my way. A part of you that understands I was making you the best agent you could be. Consider how broken up you were after the time you had together then imagine how devastated you would have been if we'd lost him in the field. So yes, I had to separate you. Tyler worked for me, after all. And he was an ambitious young man. So he dropped you when I asked him to. Quickly."

"I cried to you, Roz."

"Yes, you did. And I allowed it, didn't I?"

I ran my fingers under the edges of the coffee table. "Was it all a lie?"

She tsked. "Lyra, don't get your panties in a twist. I do care about you. All that matters to me is your success. Tyler stood in the way of that, so I eliminated the situation. It's not like I eliminated *him*, but perhaps I misled you. It was really for the best of the team and for you. And afterward, you grew and matured. I turned you into a great agent, capable of making the best calculated decisions in any given situation, even to a fault."

"You turned me into your tool. To do exactly as you wanted."

"Of course, you're my tool. After all, I was the one who trained you. Besides, where would you be without me, without The Firm?"

"You know what, that's an excellent question. I am grateful. I really am. And I really would like to return the favor. But with the recent turn of events, the circumstances, consequences, whatever you may call it, all leads me to question everything I've been told. For what it's worth, Roz, I consider you my family, so I really am trying to be fair and give you the benefit of the doubt here. But I need you to enlighten me about certain things. In fact, one very particular thing that I've been meaning to ask you since the day I found out about it. What the hell are the Renegade files?"

That was the only time I saw her mask slip. "My, my, my. Tyler is looking for a sanction, isn't he?"

"Don't bother. He's dead."

Her brows lifted. "Is he? Pity, he was a good agent. Loyal. Obedient."

I felt the sting of guilt that he was gone because of me. "That's just it. Didn't you tell him to kill me?"

Her eyes went wide. "Why on earth would I tell him to kill you?"

"Because he knew that you killed my parents."

Roz shook her head. "Not true. Tyler didn't know what happened to your parents."

"Oh, he knew. He has been collecting evidence."

"Honey, this is way above your head. I hardly know anything about your father. If Tyler's gone, it means that you saw him on your little vacation. And if he's polluted your mind with lies about me, about The Firm, consider the messenger. Haven't you been happy with me for the last five years? Haven't you grown? Haven't I given you a career, a purpose?"

"Tell me about my parents, Roz."

"I don't have anything to say. They died. The past is the past. You need to let it go."

"The past is *not* the past. *You* made it the past."

"Ah, listen to little Lyra Wilkinson. But that's not your real name, is it? Adamson? Was that the original?"

"Did you kill them?" I asked her directly.

"You're asking the wrong questions, Lyra. You always have. So, how long do I have before your little friends attempt to bust in here?"

My eyes went wide. How did she know? "I don't have any friends."

"Please. Where you go, Addie goes. And considering every time one of my men tries to eliminate you, they run into that new man of yours... What is his name? Marcus Black? Although, my dear, I must say I don't actually think he designs video games. You never were very bright."

I scowled at her. "Why would you say that to me?"

"You're just a bit naive."

"No. I came alone. I thought I could talk to you. After all, we were practically family."

Then the lights went out, and the whole house went dark.

It was only pure instinct that made me jump up and dive behind the couch before the first bullet hit the very spot where I'd been sitting.

Snipers.

Probably a long-range scope.

"Roz, this isn't the friendly conversation I'd hoped for."

"My darling Lyra, what you're going to discover over the next few minutes that you're still alive is how very, very difficult it is to kill me."

14

LYRA

Roz had been ready.

She'd been waiting for me. She knew I would come. But how?

I tapped my comm piece, and it seemed that my team was already engaging. Just because I hadn't been able to see her people didn't mean Roz had been alone. I laid some cover fire in the living room before inching to the edge of the couch and peeking my head around.

"Roz? Where are you? I just want to talk."

From somewhere near the bedroom, she called, "Talk? You came to my house with guns and backup. That doesn't look like someone who wants to talk, my darling."

In my comm piece, Rhodes's voice was clear. "Took out the sniper."

That made my job easier, and I didn't have to skulk around the house.

But clearly, she had cameras and night vision. I reached inside my jacket and pulled out my own night vision goggles. It made things easier. I wouldn't be able to see a bullet coming for me, but it was better than nothing. So there was that.

"Roz, we need to talk about my parents. About Tyler. About the assassins trying to kill me."

"Your parents were unfortunate, but losing them made you become stronger. As for Tyler, he was an important life experience you needed." Her voice was coming from the intercom now. Was she in the fucking panic room?

I inched forward. "You thought I needed to have my heart broken?"

"Well, we really wouldn't have had to move on with that exercise if you hadn't fallen for him. Honestly, I didn't know you two would hit it off so well. For the love of God, Lyra, he was a Valentine op at the time. You were bound to get your heart broken at some point."

"So what, you thought you'd expedite it?"

I cleared the house room by room. Slowly, because of the dark and the fact that I didn't know what other surprises she had in store for me. In my ear, Marcus's voice was calm. "I've taken out two by the security gate."

"You're losing your team, Roz. Just come out, and we can talk. I don't want to hurt you. I don't want to do this at all. Why did you send people after me?"

"Because you, *you* that I would have protected before anybody, you had to go and see those fucking files."

I frowned. "What files?"

There was a long, pregnant pause. And then she laughed. "You still don't know, do you?"

"Don't know what? Is it possible this has all been a horrible misunderstanding?"

With a bemused chuckle, she responded with, "Well, maybe."

"So why don't you explain what files you're talking about, and then we'll discuss if I'd misunderstood you or not?"

"My darling girl, you really can't trust anybody."

"But you said I could trust *you*. You said you would protect me from anything, didn't you?"

"God, you're so naive."

My heart started to beat faster. I knew her house well. I'd been there dozens of times over the years. I took my first steps into her bedroom and oriented myself. I knew that the panic room was down the hall to the left. The bathroom was straight ahead. And then she had a massive walk-in closet on the right. I'd gotten ready for dates in her room before.

"Roz, we don't have to do this. Just come out and talk to me."

She puffed out a harsh breath. "When are you going to see that none of this was supposed to happen this way if you had just fucking followed directions."

"Roz, I don't want to hurt you. I just want you to tell me the truth," I said, slowly walking forward.

"I want to believe you, but you're at my house with guns. None of this is what it looks like. I've only ever wanted what's best for you, Lyra."

"Great. That's what I want too. We just need to talk."

"Oh yeah? Then why do you have a silencer on your gun?"

"To be fair, a sniper tried to take me out in your living room."

And then I felt it. Stinging, searing heat grazing my shoulder.

Fuck.

"I didn't want to hurt you, Lyra. But you've really left me no choice, honestly."

"You fucking shot me."

Her chuckle was harsh. "It's a flesh wound. You'll survive."

"Roz, why would you do this?"

"This isn't about you, Lyra. It's never been about you. Why did you have to see those files?"

I still had no idea what she was talking about.

"Let's just pretend I didn't bloody see a thing, okay? For just a minute. I don't even know what I saw. Whatever you think I saw, I didn't. All I want are answers. That's it. Is that so hard?"

"Is that so hard? Do you understand how naive you are? You whine because your parents died. But didn't I give you a family? Didn't I give you a sense of belonging?"

"You did, but I can hardly forget them."

She laughed again, and it was a brutal sound. "Don't you understand? I gave you the tools to be great."

"And I'm appreciative, but tell me the truth."

"The truth would be a long time coming."

And then just as I was about to turn, something hit me on the back of the neck, and my vision went black.

MARCUS

My heart thundered in my ribcage. Behind me, Rhodes took out two more.

"Thanks," I muttered into the comms.

"Been looking out for your arse for a long time."

"It's a fine arse too."

He laughed.

"ADDIE, you're on the front of the house. Move."

Oh God, oh God, oh, God. Please, please, please. Please do not let this go bad. She'd taken a risk by coming here, but one that she thought was the right one to take. I wasn't so sure.

Addie came from around the side of the house. "Agents down. One in the corner. No Lyra."

Then I saw the taillights of a car speeding away. What the hell? Where had the car come from? No one had left the house.

Was it possible there was a tunnel in a place like this? I tapped the comms. "Lyra, come in. Lyra, come in."

But there was no response.

No. No. Bollocks, no.

I tried again. "Lyra. Come in, Lyra."

But nothing again.

Addie shook her head. "I've been through the whole house. She's not in there."

The car was a quarter of a mile down the street and gaining speed.

I glanced back at Rhodes. Then I started sprinting.

He muttered a curse and came after me. "Mate, listen. She's long gone. We have to find her another way."

"No. That bitch has her."

Addie ran after me too. She wasn't as fast as Rhodes was, but boy she was quick. "He's right. She's going to kill her."

Rhodes clamped a hand on my arm. "They have their vehicle. Ours is parked two miles out."

I tried to shake him off. "Is she tagged?"

Addie had her phone out and was checking.

She shook her head. "No. Roz might have swept her."

"Fucking hell. She hasn't activated the GPS pin in her boot?"

Addie shook her head. "No, not yet. But she's smart."

"Fuck, fuck, fuck." I jammed my hands through my hair. "We did all this so that she'd be safe. And what? We just failed?"

ADDIE'S FACE crumpled and her body sagged, but she was tossing her head back and forth. "No, no, no. Lyra's smart. She has to bide her time."

I mumbled. "Or Roz will strip her and then we'll have no idea where she is."

Addie cursed.

"Give me something. Anything," I begged.

But neither of them had anything to give. Just a whole pile of nothing.

"Nobody?" I said desperately.

Addie clapped a hand on my shoulder. "Lyra will wake up. If Roz has her, she wants her for a reason. Look, I'll go back to The Firm and grab any information I can. If Tyler was protecting her, he must have stored more information somewhere. I'll find it and bring it to you. Roz is smart, but Lyra is one of the best we have. She's going to be okay."

I slid my gaze over her. "No, there is no 'she'll be okay.' None. I told her I'd protect her, and I failed. Just like before."

I'd lost her. And worse, we never had a shot at succeeding. We'd been fucking sitting ducks the whole time, and we'd walked right into a trap. I had looked Lyra in the face, and I'd lied to her. I'd told her I would protect her, and I failed to make that happen.

15

MARCUS

When we returned to the safe house, there was no consoling me. I was going after her, period. Never mind that I had no idea where she was. She hadn't activated her GPS, and time was ticking.

All I knew was that I wanted to grab as many weapons as I possibly could, take a team back to Roz's, and go over it with a fine-tooth comb. Then I'd use any scrap of evidence to go and find Lyra.

I knew those feelings well. They'd accompanied me for a solid year after Simone. That insatiable need for revenge. Except this was worse. This feeling, overwhelmingly, was worry. What if I was too late? What if she was already gone? What if I never told her how I felt in so many words?

I'd made a pretty hefty raid on the armory at Exodus before returning to the safe house. Rhodes sat on the coffee table and watched me as I organized the guns and ammo I'd picked up. "You recognize we know nothing about where she is, who exactly has her, or what the situation is, right?"

I glowered at Rhodes. "I'm going after her."

"With what? What information?"

"I'm going to The Firm."

Rhodes stared at me incredulously. "What?"

"Whatever information I need is in that building."

"You're mad."

I shrugged. "Yeah, maybe."

"No, this is utter madness. Look, Addie is going to find the information. Lyra's gone for now, but we will get her back."

"I'm just supposed to stand around and wait for something to happen?"

"Sometimes, that's what you have to do."

I shook my head. "No, I'm not accepting that."

"But that's delusional, mate."

"Maybe, but that's what we've got going on," I said stubbornly.

"Bullshit." He tried to shove me toward my couch.

I got in his face. "What, you're going to stop me?"

Rhodes glowered at me. "I'm not going to stop you. We just need to think this through. You're not thinking clearly right now. You're a smarter agent than that."

"You don't get it, mate. This is *my* fault. We were unprepared. I let her talk me into that crazy idea. I knew it was a bad call, but I let her have her way. That's on me. I should have just tossed her over my shoulder, caveman style."

My best mate stared at me. "I know that's what you wanted to do. But think it through. There is no way on this green planet that Lyra would have let you do that. It's not on you. She's a skilled agent. She knows what the fuck she's doing."

"Oh yeah? Then why isn't she here?"

"Look, even the best agents have shit go wrong. What, you're going to act like none of us have ever gotten in a bind? Think, man. I know you want her back. I get it."

"Do you?"

"Yeah, I do actually. But we're going to do this by the book. Which means no going rogue."

"Fuck you." I tried to shove past him.

And my best mate from the first day of SAS training blocked my path. "Sorry, it's not going to happen."

"Are you out of your fucking mind?"

"Possibly. I am well aware that you would very much like to eat me for breakfast right now. And I'm sorry, but I can't let you do this. Mate, I know you want her back. I understand. I'd like you to have her back so you'll stop acting like a crazy person, but you can't do this. You can't just bulldoze your way into The Firm."

"Watch me." This time I did bump him. But I saw that he had an ace in the hole as soon as I opened the door to leave.

I found Michael waiting for me outside with four agents flanking him. He said, "Are you going to tell me where the fuck you're going with all my weapons?"

I turned back to Rhodes. "Did you do this?"

"Marcus, I'm not saying we're not going to get her, I'm just saying we're not going to do it this way."

My best mate had betrayed me.

* * *

LYRA

I woke up with a bitter taste on my tongue and my mouth feeling like I'd been chewing on a sweaty jockstrap. It took me several long seconds to realize that something was, in fact, shoved into my mouth. And then I coughed as I tried to expel it. When I spat it out, I gagged at the bitter taste of it. Oh God, I'd been drugged.

The effort to pick up my head was astronomical, let alone open my eyes. Forget the eyes. I didn't have to see for now. I just needed to get some kind of bearing on what was up and what was down. Breathing. I could focus on breathing. That's all I needed to do. In and out. No more acrid smell. No more bitter metallic taste.

"Ah, my darling girl, you're finally waking up. I was worried that we'd overdone it with the dosage."

Roz.

The kick of fury was so swift. Suddenly, I could keep my head up straight. Funny what a great motivator anger was.

"Uh-uh-uh. Easy does it. I had to give you a strong enough dose so you wouldn't see where we were. You've been out for seven hours now."

I tried to make my mouth move, but it wouldn't. It took a long moment for the brain to give the command to my lips and my tongue. And when it finally did, it came out sounding like, "Shlmshslmshlsh." I was cold too. Especially my feet. Had they taken my boots? That meant no GPS.

Roz laughed. "Ah yes, don't worry love, you can curse me out later. It's going to take a moment for the effects of the drugs to wear off. But I will unblindfold you. I need you to hold still now. I don't want to rip out any of that beautiful hair of yours."

Footsteps approached, and I tried to focus on whatever was coming. I figured Roz knew better than to come near me. I actually had better control of my limbs than I was letting on.

Subterfuge 101.

Always appear weak and helpless when you can. It makes people want to help you. And especially for someone like me, a young black woman, people are not inclined to help straight away unless I appeared helpless. Lost. Easily manipulated and malleable.

It was one of the first lessons she'd taught me. And I hadn't forgotten. When the blindfold was ripped off, it did catch in my hair. I wanted to yelp, but again, all I managed was, "Ughh."

"You fool, I told you I don't want to hurt her."

When my head lolled back into place, I finally tried the all-important open-the-eyes trick, because God, I just needed to see what the hell was going on. I peeled open my eyeballs one by one. The grit in them forced me to blink several times. Oh, God. Where the hell was I?

It was dark. Maybe underground somewhere?

"Ah yes, that's my bright girl. Trying to find out where you are. Honestly, I have to remember that I trained you myself."

I glowered at her.

"You can back off, Frank. She's not going anywhere. And she can't hurt me."

I tried to move my limbs, but she was right. I was tied down. Not that I really expected not to be, but I was still annoyed by it. "What do you want?"

"Sweetheart, you recognize that I have firmly restrained you for your own good, right? It's not my first choice, but you are a little too touchy. So until you can calm down enough that we can talk, I needed to be careful."

"I have never done anything to you."

"No. I'm not saying you have. Look, Lyra, you're like my own child. If I'd ever decided to have one, I would have wanted her to be just like you. God, you are so much like your father. You are strong and capable. And I just can't help but to be proud that I had a hand in that."

I narrowed my gaze at her. Enough bullshit. "What do you know about my father?"

She watched me carefully. "Okay, look, I wasn't entirely honest with you because those were my orders, darling. I was told not to tell you, so I didn't. But I have always regretted it. Honestly, you are such a good agent. Obviously, that's training. But you did have a natural aptitude. Your father was an excellent agent. One of the best. He trained me."

I frowned at her. "Lies." I was getting better control over my mouth.

"It's true. You were recruited because of who your father was. Also your mother, I suppose."

I went from only ever having seen my parents happy and in love, gardening and taking me to school plays and dances, to watching them die, to now being told that they were agents. It was too much to process. "No, I don't believe you." My words were still slurred.

"I'm not lying. Their code names were Rogue and Renegade." She rolled her eyes. "I mean, honestly, it's a bit on the nose, if you ask me." I didn't want to believe her, but the way she said it rang true. "He was one of the best. I was devastated when he died." The bile rose up in my throat. That part was a lie. I could tell from the way she said it.

"It's just, you know, he said he loved your mother. But he and I had an undeniable connection. There was a mission once where we had to play husband and wife. Our tension was palpable. And still, he chose your mother. I will never understand that man. He could have had me, but he chose wrong."

"So, what? You punished him because he chose my mother?"

"I wasn't *punishing* him. I just wanted him to see *me*. See what we could be together, but he kept choosing your mother."

I watched her out of the corner of my eye as she paced back and forth, and I took the opportunity to evaluate the room we were in. It actually looked kind of like our interview rooms. "What is this? An interrogation room?"

"No, darling. Of course not. Honestly, if it were up to me, I would just release you. But we need to talk first and come to an understanding."

"Fine, you're telling me my parents were these great agents. I wish I could believe you."

"Oh yes. If you could have just seen them in action. Even your mother. I'll be generous and say how good she was. See? I can be magnanimous."

I scowled at her. She was leaving something out. Most of this was true, but something wasn't right.

"When they died, I knew it was what your father would have wanted. For me to look after you."

I clanked my cuffs. "You call this looking after?"

"Ah, I know that it's not orthodox, but Lyra, you know I could never hurt you."

"No, you just send other people to do your dirty work."

Roz sniffed indignantly. "I did. I panicked. And you know what? That wasn't fair. I recognize that perhaps that was not the best way of dealing with the scenario."

"When did you come to this realization? When you tried to have me killed at the weapons auction, or when you sent a hit squad to my apartment?"

"Look, I didn't want to have to be the one to tell you. It wasn't me who you should worry about. It's Marcus."

"Just tell me the truth."

She sighed. "I know our trust is broken, but just know that I'm trying to look out for you. I'm trying to take care of you. I don't want you hurt. And this game that we're all playing, it's dangerous. I know it's hard to know who to trust, but Marcus Black is not a man you can put your faith in."

"Says the woman who tried to have me killed," I muttered.

"Love, Marcus Black has been surveilling you." Behind her was a large screen. She popped up pictures of me going to and from my apartment, to and from work. "For months now, before you were even matched on your little dating app."

I frowned. Some of the angles were taken from my apartment. But when? Had he been watching me before or after we'd been matched? "I don't believe you."

"I knew you would say that. Well, let me tell you about Marcus Black. He is the number one hitman for Exodus. He has had over a hundred and thirty-two kills. I mean, you've got what, fifty? And that was because our missions are to protect people."

I squirmed. "I don't keep count."

"Oh, well, The Firm does, love. I mean, he's just awful."

"How do you have his kill list?"

"You think we haven't been trying to stop Exodus for years now? We keep very close tabs on them. I don't blame you for being curious and having your little friends try to hack us. Just know that I am trying to keep you safe. It's what your father would have wanted."

"You keep saying that my father would have wanted this, my father would have wanted that, but I think he would have wanted me alive, too."

She frowned. "Sometimes we have to do hard things to protect the ones we love." She kept putting up more photos. Me in the gym, me going to and from work, and all those photos were taken from the front of our apartment building.

My brain tried to do a quick analysis. Addie hadn't been over much since Marcus and I were matched. So, if there were photos of her and me together, then maybe Roz was right. Maybe Marcus *was* one of the last people that I should trust.

16

MARCUS

"You want to do what?"

I glowered at Michael shortly after he and the agents he'd brought along dragged Rhodes and I back to Exodus headquarters. "I'm going after her. I don't need your permission."

He lifted a brow. "On the contrary, you don't do shit without my explicit say so."

"Fine. In that case, all that PTO you've been begging me to use, I'll just use it."

He sighed. Maggie crossed her arms and glowered at me. "So that is what's been going on in the last several days? You went after a director of The Firm without backup?"

"Yes."

"You didn't call in the team?"

I inclined my head toward Rhodes, who just stood with his back at the door, arms crossed, glaring off into space, his jaw a wall of granite. "I called *him*."

Michael said, "While he's very good, he's hardly a full team."

"This has nothing to do with Exodus. I didn't want to potentially endanger any agents and start a war," I said.

. . .

"Too late now. We've *been* at war with The Firm. You just escalated it. I'll need to take this to Command."

"Do what you want, but I'm going to get Lyra back."

Maggie sighed. "You're going after her regardless?"

I gave her a sharp nod. "Yes."

Michael crossed his arms over his chest and said, "Fine, but you're going with a team, and we're formalizing a plan. And given that the person who took her is a director of The Firm, we're going to pull up some of our notes that we have on their agency since the split."

It was my turn to clamp my jaw and do that muscle-ticking thing. They were wasting time.

Michael could read the disdain in my expression and said, "That's the only way we're letting you out of here. So take it or leave it."

I scowled at him. I already had a plan. Break into The Firm and make someone tell me where they were hiding her.

Oh yeah, real solid plan.

He laughed. "Take as long as you need."

"The hell—"

"Might I remind you, you're already on very thin ice. There are only two reasons I'm letting this shit go. One is because you're one of the best, and two, you may have actually found a terrorist cell. So give us some time to prep for this. In the meantime, you said you have a Firm agent involved in this. Call her in. We'll see what we can get from her."

"With every minute that ticks by, Lyra is in more danger."

Michael leaned in and lowered his voice. "This isn't like the Simone situation."

I expected more of a sting, but hearing her name was more like a dull ache. It still hurt, but it was more like the phantom pain of an old injury. Nothing compared to the fear I felt because of the possibility of losing Lyra and repeating the Simone situation all over again. "I'm not saying it is."

"I know that no matter what, the loss of her is still fresh. I understand that. I don't want to see that happen to you again. We will do this together. *Teamwork*. Remember how that goes?"

"Make it happen, or I will bust out of here and go get her my goddamn self."

"I hear you. Now, give us a little time."

He turned his attention to Rhodes. "Get that girl from The Firm in here."

Rhodes just nodded. "Yeah, on it."

As I followed Rhodes out of the briefing room, I muttered to him. "Sod you, mate. Thanks for nothing."

He frowned. "You're a dick. I love you, too."

"I just need her back."

"Just as long as you don't do something stupid again. I'll follow you anywhere."

"Apparently, not *anywhere*."

He rolled his eyes. "You were going to do something stupid."

"I'm not stupid."

"Uh-huh, and it's my job to step in and say, mate, you're being a knob."

I gave him a brisk nod. "Yeah, let's get Addie in here. I don't want to lose any more time."

"Roger that."

There was a feeling settling in my chest. One that I couldn't quite identify. But it felt an awful lot like relief. Michael was right. I didn't have any idea how I was going to get Lyra back. I just wanted to run in headfirst. But that would likely get her killed. And to get her back, I knew I was going to need every single one of my resources.

MARCUS

An hour later, we had Addie with us, and she filled us in on what she knew.

"All right. With Roz out, I wasn't sure who knew what, so I stayed away from the office. William Browning is in charge when she is not there. I suppose I could have gone to him, but I didn't know who to trust."

I gave her a nod. "Okay, what did you find out about Roz and her whereabouts?"

She shook her head. "I haven't. She's ghosted, and I need to be careful about who I ask. I did go back to Roz's house and sort through what was left in her safe room. There are records of some accounts. A folder full of them. I've got my computer processing them now. They looked like Swiss bank accounts as far as I can tell, all in her parents' names. There are some letters, some photographs, nothing of much use. And I don't have clearance to poke around properly."

Rhodes grinned at her. "Well, you won't be needing any clearance for what we're about to do."

"What he means is, we're going to break into the Firm," I said.

She laughed. "Are you insane? The place is crawling with agents. Anybody who doesn't belong there is going to get shot."

"Well, that's why we're going to have you on the inside."

"You've got to be kidding. My entire career will be at stake."

"This isn't for you, for me, or anyone else. This is to get Lyra back. Or don't you want that?"

She stared at me. "You know I want that. But there has to be a way to do it safely. And I don't think me walking in there is going to cut it."

"Let me break it down for you, princess, if we don't break in there, your boss, or former boss, or whatever she is, will kill Lyra. Right now, we have no way of tracking her, no way of identifying where she is, nothing. I can't let it go. I need some answers. Answers that are going to come from inside the building you work in. You saw what happened when Roz let loose. She's going to know you helped Lyra. How long do you think they'll let you live?"

I knew I was being a little too harsh. But one, I was not even sure if Lyra was still alive, so I didn't give a shit about anything else right now. Two, if I had to manipulate Addie into helping, then I would. Whatever I needed to do to get the job done and bring Lyra home.

"Well, you're a piece of work," she said.

"Yes, I know. But all I care about right now is bringing her back. So you can think I'm a wanker later."

"What was that word Rhodes called you before? A knob? I like that."

"Fine. Call me whatever you like. Let's just get this show on the road, shall we?" I pulled out a map of the streets surrounding P.O.P. PR & Marketing. "How the hell do we get into this fortress?"

She smiled. "You walk in the front door."

17

LYRA

When I woke again, Roz was kneeling in front of me. "Ah, there you are. Ready to talk now?"

I swallowed hard. "Are you ready to let me go?"

"I'm not holding you prisoner, Lyra. I'm trying to *protect* you."

I bit the inside of my cheek. I knew about the surveillance. I still couldn't believe it though. The ways people lied in an attempt to manipulate me was astounding. Did everyone think I was stupid?

"Clearly, I have a problem with trust. I keep putting it in the wrong people."

"It's not your fault. Honestly, it's mine, love. I brought you in too young. You probably needed another year, a little seasoning before I started training you. I was just trying to honor your parents' wishes."

I scowled at all the monitors with Marcus's pictures on them. "None of it was real, was it?"

Roz shook her head. "No, it wasn't. And I owe you an apology, I know. I should never have interfered with your relationship with Tyler. I thought I was moving your training further along. I didn't know you were going to get hurt that badly."

"How were you supposed to know?" I could play along. Let her think all of her bullshit was working.

"Exactly. Probably like every mother before me, at some point I thought that I was doing the right thing. And I was mistaken."

"Can we just do away with these?" I lifted my arms and jangled my cuffs.

She tsked at me. "We both know full well you can get out of those on your own."

I glanced up at her and then at the corners of the room for the surveillance that I couldn't see but knew was there. "What, no one is going to run in and shoot me?"

She pressed her lips together in firm disappointment. "Like I said, you're not a prisoner."

"You could have fooled me."

"I just wanted you restrained long enough to show you what you needed to see. What I'm doing here is to protect people like you."

"What exactly *are* you doing here, Roz?"

"First free yourself, then come and see."

When I saw that she was serious and no one was going to put a hole in my forehead, I made a couple of quick flicks of my wrist and I was free. Just like she'd shown me years ago.

While I rubbed my wrists, she leaned down and encompassed me in a hug. "I'm so glad you can see things properly now, Lyra."

"You want to tell me where we are?" I didn't hug her back.

"Come on. On your feet. You probably need to stretch your legs. You've been stuck sitting here for so long."

"Yeah, you could say that."

"Come on."

We stepped out of the white room and into a well-lit

hallway that felt light and airy, yet somehow still subterranean. "Where are we?"

"This is a facility I've had for some years. It's off-grid. Why do you think I married Adam in the first place? His family has properties all over Los Angeles. It wasn't very difficult to get access to one and have it deeded to myself. He didn't even realize it. The power of love, I suppose."

"And where is Adam?"

"Europe or somewhere? I don't know. I really don't keep tabs on him. It's for the best."

"Right. So he's not involved with whatever you have going on?"

"What? Are you kidding? He's not bright enough, and he lacks the vision and the stomach needed to make a difference."

"Of course." All I could do was nod and smile.

"I know that sounds unkind, and I don't mean it to be. It's just we each have very specific things that we take care of, and this isn't on his need-to-know list."

I followed along behind her, and all along the way, people in uniform greeted her with a nod and a salute.

She was most definitely in charge. "And what is this place?"

"This is a project I've been working on a very long time."

"What is the purpose and objective?"

"Lyra, I know this can be hard to hear, but The Firm has been ineffectual for too long. Their methods need revamping. They've grown old and stale. It's time for new blood. A new organization. We're at the point where we can make real change and actually help people. People who need our help that the system says we shouldn't help. I think it's wrong."

"Okay, but I'm still not exactly sure what the goal is."

"The goal is money. I want to be able to help the most vulnerable. You don't know it, but The Firm makes choices about who deserves their help and who doesn't."

"Okay."

The glint in her eye warned me to tread carefully.

What? More than the bat shit crazy she's spewing?

"The wrong kind of people prosper."

"It's an imperfect system, Roz. You always said that."

"Yes, it is imperfect. But *I* can do it better. And not all terrorist organizations are created the same. There are some that want to make changes. There are some that are actually trying to help people. They are more freedom fighters, really."

My stomach roiled. "Roz, their methods..."

She reached out and touched my arm. "Ah, methods. Sometimes we need a little violence to get a point across."

"That's never been what you believed."

"Well, maybe that's what I believe now. I'm tired of watching the wrong people slither out from under retribution."

I shook my head. "You always said that violence was not the answer."

"I know. And it's not. But ugh, sometimes it can be so sweet."

"That's vengeance, Roz."

"And sometimes vengeance and retribution are what's needed."

"You have never thought that. In fact, you've always tried to teach me just the opposite."

"Well, maybe I think it now." She paused. "Maybe if I had been thinking about that before, people like your father would still be alive."

Ah, she was finally getting to the piece of information that I wanted. "Can you tell me more about my father?"

"Of course, dear. But first, let me show you something."

And then I watched in horror as I was led into a long, expansive room. Again, all white. I sensed a theme.

On one end was a strikingly familiar weapon. On the other

end was some kind of chamber. It was manned by someone, and then... Oh my God, was someone in there?

"Roz, what's happening here?"

"Ah, yes, that's Logan Brodick. Your little human trafficker friend. The one who had the girl at the compound." She waved her hand.

"Yes, I know who that is. But The Firm didn't apprehend him."

"No. *They* didn't apprehend him, but my people did. Again, The Firm was ineffectual. Now that I have him, we're going to serve up a little retribution."

I stared at her. "Roz, he belongs in jail. His victims deserve justice."

"Oh no, jails are ineffective. People like him still prosper. Still run their little games from prison. I'm making sure that the likes of him never get out on the street."

"What?"

And then, in my wide-eyed terror, the lab tech in all-white turned on the weapon.

I turned my head away as Brodick's scream filled the air. Oh, God. The bile came rushing up so quickly, I worried about not making it to a wastebasket. But then one of her men placed a tin basket under me as I vomited into it.

"Oh my God."

"Oh, Lyra. I never did understand you. On the one hand, you happily kill bad guys. On the other hand, you act as if this is beneath you. Either you are born for the revolution, or you're not."

"You're murdering people, Roz."

"Oh, relax. That's because we've been paid to. I no longer have to try and use him to try and get to someone larger. It was my job to get rid of him. And since we are now in possession of the weapon, I had to demonstrate that it works. Not to worry. We're not going to let the weapon get back out on the streets. But it is ours to use as we see fit."

I frowned as everything came into a glaring clarity. "Prochenko, he works for you?"

Roz sighed. Then smiled sheepishly. "Okay, fine, he does."

"That night I was almost mugged, you sent him to kill me?"

"Naughty me. Yes. But you'd seen the schematics of this facility. I couldn't risk you piecing everything together."

My stomach churned. "I didn't know what I'd seen."

"I did eventually realize that. You weren't acting boastful but rather afraid. If it helps, I am sorry." A tear fell down her cheek.

"Are you?"

I knew then that all those years ago I'd made a terrible mistake. I should never have trusted her. But now it was too late.

MARCUS

Addie hadn't been kidding when she said we'd walk in the front door. Rhodes and I went in the front door, literally, as a cleaning crew.

He scowled down at the outfit. "I'm British SAS, at Her Majesty's bloody service. And now I'm part of a cleaning crew?"

I frowned at him. "Hey, it's the job."

"But I'm an assassin for the love of Christ."

"Yes, I know. You're an assassin, but buckle up. Where do you think you'd be now if we didn't have cleaners come and clean up your little messes?"

He blinked at me. "Jail. You know I'm too good looking for jail, right?"

I snorted. "Right."

Addie, who'd gone in ahead of us, met us at the door. "If you two are done with the witty banter, I have temporarily disabled the cameras. You've got thirty seconds to get in here."

We didn't waste time. We were in full cleaning gear, just like the regular cleaning crew. The same cleaning crew that Rhodes and I called off an hour ago. That had been an easy hack. Break into the system, tell them P.O.P. was canceling for the night due to an event. Easy. Then we showed up.

Since we didn't have actual credentials, Addie was letting us in. "It's this way. There are cameras in the hallways, but you have a viable reason to be in the records room. It's just a quick clean, so you'll have less than five minutes. If you can't find whatever you need in that time, you'll have to get out because lingering will be suspicious."

Rhodes slid his gaze over her. "What will you be doing?"

"I will be in Roz's office. I'm going to try and find something, *anything,* that might tell us where they are. Lyra needs us."

Once we had the directions to where we were going, walking through P.O.P. Marketing was fairly easy. It looked like every other marketing company. The kind you see on TV. Cubicles, brightly colored posters that contained actual marketing campaigns. I wondered if the people who marked up that nonsense knew where they actually worked, the shadow of it all. But at the end of the day, they weren't that different than we were.

Except you don't have a homicidal maniac running your team.

Well, one never knew about Maggie, but Michael was solid. He genuinely cared about the team. He wanted to see us do well.

When we reached the records room Addie had pointed us

to, we abandoned the cart and I kneeled in front of the lock, placing my decryption device over it.

He was keeping an eye on his watch and the cameras. We had another ten, nine, eight, seven, six...

Before we hit five, the decryption device flashed green, the door unlocked and swung in, and Rhodes followed me inside. We left the cart out in the hallway in case anyone was curious about the movement inside the room. Once we got access, we got to work. Rhodes might not have been as good with computers as I was, but he wasn't helpless. He could deal with elementary things, look ups, research.

"Any idea what we're looking for?"

"I'll look for Lyra's parents. You look for Tyler Warden."

"Got it."

We both checked our watches, knowing exactly how much time we had left. It was not that long. And I hoped to God Lyra was okay. When I sat down, I managed to bypass several initial firewalls with Addie's login credentials. And once I was in, I was able to spoof the system into thinking it was Roz logging in, which was good because she had access to a lot of things that Addie didn't.

Then I hunted down any information I could find on Lyra Adamson. She'd grown up just outside of Western Massachusetts, in a little town called Shrewsbury. Her father was some kind of engineer. Her mother a fashion designer. At least that's what it said on paper.

But Lyra had gone to private schools most of her life and traveled around the world with her parents. Interesting spots like Prague, Thailand, and Russia. All hot spots in our line of work. Were those trips actually missions?

Don't get distracted. Focus on what you need. Lyra is depending on you.

I found all the basics. Her parents died when she was eighteen, and then Lyra was approached to join The Firm at nineteen. I went back to her parents again and typed in their names. Her mother's name got flagged first.

Helen Adamson, maiden name, Darfoor.

She'd been born in Ghana, but then raised in the States in the DC area. She'd gone to Boston College where she'd met John Adamson and they had fallen in love.

It was all a great story.

But, when I tried to research Boston College for records of Helen Adamson, I came up empty.

A quick search told me that she'd worked at a company called HD Accra Fashions and further digging led me to BH. That was the Boston location of the Firm. As for her husband... John Adamson didn't work for Blakely Tech. Blakely Tech didn't exist. He, in fact, also worked for The Firm.

Holy cow, both of her parents were Firm agents, after all. And Lyra had no idea about any of it.

"Did you find anything?"

"Yeah. I found a lot, actually. Both of her parents were Firm agents just like Tyler's flash drive indicated. Code names, Renegade and Rogue. One daughter. Lyra. When she was sixteen, they were asked to put her on track for Firm training, and they declined. They didn't want her to be an agent." I knew Exodus's history indicated that was one of the key points our founders had disagreed upon. Aiden Saint-James had wanted to recruit agents at a very young age. Orion McClintock prefer to use ex-military.

"So she got her badassery from them."

"Yeah, she certainly did."

"Mate?"

I glanced up at him. "I know. We're out of time."

I downloaded everything that I could, making sure to back myself out and log both Roz and Addie out of the system.

"Do you have what we need on Tyler?"

He nodded. "I got it."

"Let's go."

We eased out of the records room, taking our time and whistling like regular cleaning staff. There was one agent still at a desk that we passed. He nodded his thanks and then frowned for a moment. "Are you guys new?"

Rhodes gave him one of his killer smiles. "Yup. Angus and Rey were absent, so we got called in."

He laughed. "Ah yes, Angus said they were trying to have a baby, so I guess that's how sick they are."

I was relieved that it was standard protocol for us to do full research on anyone we'd be replacing, because that could have gone poorly.

When we found Addie, she was waiting for us at the front door. "You got everything you need?"

We nodded and she held up a folder. "Me too. The good news is, I know where Lyra is. The bad news is, it's going to be a bitch to get her out."

"Good thing we have the entire Exodus team ready to go."

Her brows shot up. "Lyra is not Exodus."

"No." I shook my head. "She's not. But Exodus isn't interested in her. They're gunning for Roz because the people she's working with are some of the biggest terrorists that we've been after for years. Make no mistake, Exodus is helping us, but they're not entirely altruistic."

Addie shook her head. "I don't even care at this point. I just want my best friend back."

"Me too. Me too."

18

LYRA

My mother used to have a saying that everybody knows which one of their friends is most likely to be a homicidal maniac.

Roz was that friend, and I couldn't believe that I hadn't seen it before. For the last six years, she'd been the person that I went to for everything. She was not my mother, but she was certainly the closest thing I'd had to one after my mom's death. Or so I'd thought.

As she walked me around her little house of horrors, she showed off proudly, and I couldn't help but think back to every single lecture I'd ever gotten from her about how we couldn't just kill people and how everyone has a purpose. I'd seen no less than three of the men I'd worked for years to put away, people that had always just slipped out of our fingers, who were at her facility and working for her. The horror in realizing that she'd been helping them for her own reasons, for her own cause, made me sick. But more importantly, the fact that I'd been so naive that I'd blindly followed her. What she was doing now made all the years I spent with The Firm seem like a lie. She'd made a mockery of my whole life, because if I left, what job could I have now?

You'd be free.

Sure, I could go do something else. Join a real government agency, because the truth of it was, all I knew about The Firm was what she'd told me. What if I'd been working for the bad guys all along like Marcus had suggested? Was he even alive? Was Addie? My twisted pool of feelings about them was not going to get me out of there.

You need to focus. You need to think.

One of Roz's little minions had put me in what they called the guest room. Well lit, furnished decently, though minimally. And there was a couple of bright pops of color in potted orchids. Roz had always loved orchids. But there were no windows. And having already tried the door, I knew that wasn't a viable way out. The only way I was getting out of there was when Roz was damn well good and ready to let me out.

I had become her prisoner again. She hadn't quite enjoyed my response to her little weapons demonstration. So there was that.

I needed to find a way out. I tried to turn on the GPS signal in my boots, but I knew we were underground, so having no signal wasn't a surprise.

Think it through, Lyra. The only way she's going to let you out to roam around is if you say you agree with her and that you don't give a hoot about human life. That's how you're going to save yourself.

I was still reeling from the things she'd said about my parents. She'd known them. Was she the reason they were gone? That idea scared me. She'd known my parents, knew who they really were, but she'd barely shared anything about them. And every time she did, only bits and pieces of information were mentioned. It almost seemed like she was keeping something very significant from coming out.

I'd been completely lost after they died, only to find out that I walked right into the life that they'd chosen. Had they wanted this for me? Had that been their plan all along? All I had to go on was Roz's word.

When the door opened, I glanced up from the bed. I smiled up at the woman that came in with a tray of food. "Hi, I'm Lyra."

She gave me a nod.

"Um, what's your name?"

"Natasha."

Her voice was soft, with a drowsy tone that made me want to immediately relax, even though I knew better. "Nice to meet you, Natasha. Listen, is it possible that I can see Roz?"

She shook her head. "No, there's a meeting. When she's finished though, I'll send her in to you."

"Do you mind sitting with me? This is all really new, and it's taking me some time to adjust. I just don't want to be by myself."

She studied me. "You're the one."

My brow furrowed. "The one what?"

Her smile was soft. "The daughter Roz speaks of."

If that was supposed to reassure me, it certainly did not. "Oh, I'm not her actual daughter."

She frowned. "She said that you were."

"Uh, maybe I'm *like* a daughter to her. But I'm not adopted or anything."

She gave me a shy smile. "I had wondered."

It was then that I recognized her accent. Estonian maybe? "How did Roz find you?"

"Clive Moran is my father."

Over the years, I'd been working on perfecting my poker face. Thank God. Because she'd unknowingly dropped a bomb on me. This was Clive Moran's daughter? Forced into work in this underground bunker for Roz?

Moran was the head of Signat. They'd been active for nearly thirty years. Jesus, had Roz always been bad?

"Are you and your father close?"

She shook her head. "No. But he and my mother were having a custody fight. He took me and brought me here. He and Roz are, I don't know, together?"

"Natasha, do you want to be here?"

She studied me. It was a battle of wills between us because neither one of us could trust the other. After all, we could both report each other to Roz, and then where would we end up?

"I wish I saw sunlight. Don't say I said that."

And then I took a leap of faith. "And your mother?"

A quick shuttering of her eyes told me what I needed to know. She didn't want to be there. She was not there by choice. She was there for survival.

"Look, if you just let me out, I can try and get us out of here."

"You don't know my father. He won't allow it."

"Maybe, but we have to try, right? You have to realize you're not leaving here if you don't take action."

"Roz wanted you here. Once she realized she couldn't kill you, she said it was more important to have you here instead of out there poking around her business."

"Right, because my mentor has been trying to kill me."

She winced. "I am sorry. That is probably horrible to hear."

"No. The truth is the truth. It can't hurt you, right?"

She nodded. "Yes. I'm still sorry though."

"It's fine. And your father essentially imprisoned you here, so that's equally terrible."

"Yes, it is."

"So what are we going to do about it?"

"You think you alone can break us out of here?" she scoffed. "We're underground. Do you know how long she's been building this place?"

"No, why don't you tell me?" I eyed the food on the plate. "Is that poisoned?"

"Don't drink the cola. That has been drugged. The water is clean."

I blinked at her honesty. "Thank you."

"You're the first person I can actually talk to in here. Everyone else believes in Roz's cause and my father's."

I hated to ask but knew I had to. "Roz's husband, Adam, where is he?"

Natasha frowned then. "What does he look like?"

I furrowed my brow trying to think how to describe him. "About five-ten, has a paunch, salt and pepper hair, kind eyes."

Natasha winced. "Oh, he died a month ago. What she did to him, it wasn't in kindness."

"Right. Okay, let's get out of here."

"How?"

"I don't know how yet," I said, "but at least get me out of this room so that I can have a look around the facility. Scope it out, case it, find the chinks in the system."

"You're going to have to learn to lie better."

I nodded. "Yeah. The throwing up thing certainly did not help."

"She doesn't trust you, you know. Which is why she's drugging you."

"Right. Thank you for the warning."

She nodded. "It's the least I can do. But I'm not a soldier."

"No, you're not. But not everyone needs to be. And I have friends. Can you get access to a phone?"

She shook her head. "The only access to the outside world is hard wired. You can tap in and use the internet if you want but only some sites, and they're all monitored."

I sighed. "How many stories down are we?"

"Six."

"Is there an elevator? Stairs?"

"There are stairs and an elevator. They're all guarded though."

"Right." I touched her arm, attempting to show her my concern. "Listen Natasha, I appreciate your help. And don't you worry. I'm going to get you out of here. I promise."

"How are you going to do that?"

"I don't know yet, but just know that as devious as Roz is, she trained me. I will find a way to get you out of here."

***

LYRA

The next morning, or at least I thought it was morning, there was someone at my door again, and I sat up, hoping for another opportunity to get out, look around, escape.

It was Natasha again. And as much as I wanted to get out, I wanted to make sure I protected her too. She was just as much a victim as I was. "You're back."

"Yeah, um, I wanted to see how you were. I was going to bring you more food, but Ivan beat me to it. He's mostly fine. Sort of harmless, really. But don't drink whatever he put in front of you. The coffee will smell good, but it will knock you out again."

"Thanks."

"You still have your bottle of water under the bed?"

I nodded. "I've been filling it with the tap water from the sink."

"Okay, good." She went to back away, and I stopped her.

"Wait. I need to figure a way to get out of here."

She looked down the hall. "I might be able to say I'm taking you to the gym for a workout?"

"Anything. I will be quick."

"All right. Come along."

"Thank you," I said, grateful to be making some progress with the frightened girl.

"Has Roz been here to see you?"

I shook my head. "No, but at this point, I didn't really expect her to come. She knows me well enough to know that I was disgusted and horrified by what she was doing and who she was working with. She hasn't been buying my little charade. Matter of fact, she may even be playing me. Where's the gym?"

"This way." And then she leaned in and whispered, her lips barely moving, perhaps to keep the cameras from catching her. "Around it is an elevator. You can try and use it to get outside, but do so at your own peril."

"Noted."

She hadn't been kidding about the gym. When I peered in the glass windows, everything I saw was state-of-the-art equipment, everything brand new and shiny. How long had Roz been planning this? All those times she and Adam had traveled, but this wasn't a just-now thing. This was a situation she'd carefully thought about for years. She wouldn't have been able to scam enough from missions, steal enough from assets, or siphon enough from Adam to fund all of this. Someone had paid her well. I needed to find out who.

"Thank you for this." I said.

She shrugged. "Sure thing."

"You're going to be okay, right?"

"Sure, I'm perfectly fine."

Knowing that was usually code for, 'hell no, I'm not fine at all,' I said, "You can come with me."

"I'm pretty sure if I go anywhere, my father will have my mother killed. That's if she's even still alive."

"So what, you'll just stay down here like a prisoner?"

She hung her head. "Maybe. I just know I'm not ready."

"That's no way to live."

"No one can protect her, not from him."

I sighed, because she might be right. The kind of people

Roz was in bed with meant any tussling with them was going to get people dead.

Suddenly the lights flickered, and Natasha froze.

I asked her, "What is that? Why do you look like that?"

"The silent alarm has been tripped. Someone's here."

"What does that mean? Tell me what's happening."

"I don't know. But we've got to get you back to your cell," she said with obvious fright in her voice.

"Oh, no. No. I'm not going back to the cell. You might as well tell me what's happening."

"I don't know. But if you go back to your cell, I can find out and let you know."

I shook my head. "If I go back in that cell, I might never come back out again."

"I've only ever seen this happen once when someone tried to escape."

"So escape is possible?"

She frowned at me then. "No one has ever done it successfully."

"Oh, God. Way to give me a false sense of optimism."

"Sorry."

"Show me the elevator. I'll do it myself."

"You'll be killed. You don't know where to go, and now that the silent alarm has been triggered, everyone is on red alert. Go back to your cell," she demanded.

I shook my head. "Sorry, Natasha, I can't."

"I will die when they discover I helped you."

"Your father went so far as to bring you here, so he's not going to let anything happen to you." I prayed I wasn't wrong.

"But he can punish me through my mother."

Bile rose in my throat as I thought of that. I turned and glanced longingly at that corner corridor that would lead to my potential freedom. And there was a part of me that didn't want to listen. That didn't want her to be right. But I knew if I continued on this path, the girl would likely die. If not physically, then part of her heart would. All because I couldn't be patient. "Okay, fine, let's go back."

Visibly relieved, she led me back down the hall toward my cell while guards and agents ran toward the direction we'd come from. When we rounded the next turn to get back to the room, there was a movement in one of the doorways that caught my attention. Blond bouncy curls. I frowned. Addie?

I ran ahead of Natasha then.

There was no way Addie was there. No. She didn't know about this. Did she tip Roz off?

Natasha caught me by the arm when I tried to run past my room. "Nope, in here. I'm sorry, but it's not safe right now."

I ground my teeth. "No, there was a woman down the hall that I think I know."

Addie. Had she come for me?

I wanted to keep arguing with her, but then I looked down. She had a gun in her palm. I frowned up at her. "Natasha?"

"I don't want to use this, but you need to go back in."

I put my hands up.

"I'm sorry. But if you try to escape right now, there will be nothing I can do to help you. And I can't let that happen." She unlocked my room and then shoved me backward into it. "I'm sorry."

The door closed with an audible click as the heavy lock re-engaged. I leaned my forehead against the door and sagged, tears welling in my eyes. Fuck, I should have just fought her. She looked like a kid, but that might be part of the game. How the hell was I going to get out of here now?

19

MARCUS

I studied the nondescript building three miles ahead through the high-powered binoculars. "That's it? Doesn't look like much."

Addie was right by my side. "That's because it's meant to look that way. Nothing special in a pseudo-residential-industrial area. What's really important is the network underground that you can't see." She took the blueprints and laid them out in front of us. "This is the facility." She pointed out the eastern corner. "This is the most secure area. We've got maps in our tablets to lead us there. The reason I say that Lyra's probably there is it's the most defensible area."

"And if she's not there?"

"Then we are shit out of luck. Because that's the best spot. That's where I'd put her if I was a homicidal maniac."

I could almost laugh at that, but then I sobered. What must it be like for them, knowing that their mentor was just this side of crazy? That they'd dedicated their lives to something that had been a lie, if not from the start, then at least for the last several years. How many people had they killed following orders, and how many of those orders had been *true* orders?

I shook my head. "Addie, are you okay?"

She blinked at me. "I don't understand the question."

I picked up the binoculars and began assessing where the cameras were. "I just know how close you two were."

"Are. How close we *are*. And yeah, I want her back. More importantly, I want to make sure no one gets hurt. Especially Lyra, but none of us either."

I nodded. "No one's getting hurt. Not today."

"Well, Roz has already proven that she doesn't really give a fuck about anyone else. So I'd like to knock it dead because I have a whole vengeance scheme planned out."

I smiled at that. "You were hurt by her too."

"Hell yeah. She's been a mentor to all of us. It sucks."

I nodded. "Yeah, it must."

On the comms, Maggie and Michael were listening and doling out orders.

"Team four, you are west side. We want live capture of all agents that come flooding out of there. Team three, north side. You will go first and make way for teams one and two," Michael said.

Maggie followed up. "Team two, when they're in, clear a path and see if there are additional hostages. Wait for your clearance from teams four and three before you move forward."

The adrenaline was humming under my veins. I could feel her. She was in there.

I just had to find her.

I just wanted her back safe and sound, and I would tell her that no one was going to hurt her again. That she was safe with me.

Is that even true?

It was sort of the truth.

As long as you're an agent, she will always be in danger.

I shoved that thought aside. I didn't have time for it. All I had time for was going in there and getting her back alive. We'd figure out the rest later.

In our comm units, Maggie's voice was clear. "Team one, proceed."

Addie looked at me and nodded her head. We packed up our surveillance gear and piled in the van.

Once we were a mile out, we parked again, loaded up with weapons strapped on our backs and our hips and our legs, and we moved in.

I might not understand Addie being affiliated with The Firm as a general rule, but I had to say she was a good agent. When it came to the work, she was decisive and fast. Didn't kick up a fuss. Did what needed to be done. Just like any of our agents.

She'd been well trained. And she had that single-minded focus of someone who'd taken many orders and who knew how to fight for what was important.

When teams three and four reported that they'd taken out the cameras and dealt with the guards, we went in through the east side of the building. The power was already out on that side of the property, but we disarmed the cameras there, nonetheless. Addie was fast with the infrared, and then we padded slowly inside, ready and willing to do what we needed to do, but so far, we'd met no resistance.

When we reached the security panel, Addie set up her decryption device, and I placed my hand over it. At first it just flashed red. And then after several seconds, green. The elevator doors opened. It was well-lit, bright. I knew that it would take me to Lyra, and that was all I cared about. I glanced at Addie. "I guess I'm ready if you are."

She grinned at me. "I was born ready."

I groaned "Oh no, you're not going to start with the bad movie quotes, are you?"

She laughed. "What, Lyra didn't tell you? I love a cheesy movie quote. I can do this all day."

I leaned my head back against the elevator after I checked the safety on my gun. "Something tells me this is going to be a long afternoon."

"You can say that again."

LYRA

Just a little further.

If I could just reach that damn panel. Just under the camera in the corner, there was an electronic panel, and I was hoping I could short it out and open the damned door. I had no weapons, which was a problem, sure. But I'd cross that bridge later. All I knew was that I couldn't stay in my cell. I had no friends in here, so best to get the hell out.

I pulled over my cot to stand on and began to slowly turn the screws and pray. I didn't care if my fingers bled, bruised, and turned sensitive from my attempts to free myself.

I couldn't give up.

Even if Roz was on the other side of that door ready to barge in, I had to do this. So far, I'd been able to hear when someone was coming, but with the alarm blaring, it might be different.

Fortunately, I was able to loosen the first screw before I heard footsteps outside the door. I hopped down, dragging my cot back with quickness and efficiency.

Quickly, I threw myself on the bed, turning around to see the door open. With the screw between my fingers as a weapon, I pretended I was asleep. Maybe if I got the jump on someone, I'd be able to surprise them with my weapon and get out.

As the footsteps slowly approached, I forced myself to take

a deep breath. The intent in situations like this was to use the element of surprise, otherwise it could get you hurt. That meant you didn't get to escape.

So I was loosey-goosey. My plan was to get out of there, and whoever this was approaching me wasn't going to make it through the night.

I could feel the movement, the body heat. A hand brushing over me, drawing closer. And I waited, biding my time. As soon as there was contact, I rolled and lunged up, sending my fist straight for the jugular, but the move was deflected. I swept my legs out and around, hitting them just at the knee, and there was a grunt.

And then a familiar voice said, "Lyra, it's us. Stand down."

Addie?

I didn't stop though. Even though Addie's voice was crystal clear, like I was talking to her in the office, I still lunged my whole body despite my lack of strength and the earlier drugs still making their way through my system. Fists up, I was ready to jam that screw into a temple. But an arm went up, blocking me easily and then wrapped around my shoulders, attacking me back to front.

I wiggled. "Let me go."

"No. It's me. You're safe. You are always safe in my arms, Lyra. I would never hurt you."

And then I froze. Marcus. He'd come for me.

I wanted to believe. I wanted to trust that it was his voice. My gaze flew to the side, and I wanted to believe that it was Addie I saw. But what if it was a trick? What if I was still drugged? What if this was some kind of fiction? Oh, God.

And then the Addie imposter whipped up her balaclava, and I could see her blond curls swept back in a ponytail. "See? It's me."

Suddenly, all the fight seeped out of my bones, and I was jelly. Melting.

Marcus held me up. "I've got you. You're okay. Nothing's going to happen to you."

"You came for me."

He leaned down and kissed the shell of my ear softly. "Hell yes, we did."

I turned in his arms and slid my hands up to his face, my fingertips tracing along as I slid his balaclava partway off. "Oh, God, it's you."

He nodded slowly, and I could see his lopsided smile. "Yeah, I told you. No matter what, I'll always come for you."

Another wave of relief made my knees buckle again. "Oh, God, I'm so happy to see you."

"You're okay?" Marcus's hands did a quick check over me. It was perfunctory. Tactical. Meant to assess if I had any injuries, but that didn't stop the heat from trailing over me.

When I gasped as he searched my ribs, his gaze met mine, and he smirked.

Arsehole.

"We'll have time for that later, he said with a chuckle.

"Yeah. Now, someone hand me a fucking gun."

Addie grinned as she unstrapped several magazines and a gun from her back. "Are your hands okay to shoot?"

"Just fine. And I have some people that I would like to pay back, please."

Addie consulted a tablet of some sort. "Okay, let's go."

"Dare I ask where we got this fancy equipment?"

Marcus grinned. "There are some perks of being with me and my guys. My whole team is here. All to bring you home."

Home. That was a funny word. I had no idea what that even meant to me now. The woman who trained me, turned me into an agent, for so many years she'd *been* my home, my anchor point, my safe space. But as it turned out, there was nothing safe about her. She'd been the wolf in sheep's clothing all along, and I hadn't known.

"I don't care where we're going, just get me the fuck out of here."

He grinned. "Roger that." Then he sobered and cursed under his breath. "I couldn't figure out why you didn't activate the GPS until we had to take that long elevator ride to find you."

"When I first got here, I would have, but I was drugged and not thinking clearly. Then I woke up and realized this place was subterranean, and there was no signal so I couldn't activate the GPS. But let's go. Get me out of here. We'll talk about it when we're out."

"Good." Marcus handed me a comm unit and I slipped it in my ear.

Knowing he wouldn't have been left out of this mission, I said, "Rhodes, are you there somewhere?"

There was almost a happy tone in Rhodes's voice. "Ah, the lady of the hour. You're done lazing about? Ready to get some bad guys?"

"Bro, you know I've already killed dozens."

He chuckled. "You wish. You should catch up, Lyra."

"I intend to."

I barely knew Rhodes. We'd been fighting together for what, a few days? A week? But already, he felt familiar. Kind of like family.

Be careful how easily you use that family term.

We made a left at the end of the hallway and passed where I'd last seen Natasha. I wanted to stop. Go and get her. Tell her there was a way out.

And then I remembered she'd shoved me back in the room. So maybe it was best to leave her on her own.

We made it up and down another set of hallways. All the while, Addie was consulting the map. Finally, we made a left. "Okay, we're coming to the place where we need to be more careful. It's the fastest way out, so we'll just—"

"Well, well, well... if it isn't two of my protégés and what I can only assume is an Exodus agent. I should probably mention you two are fired, right?"

I slowly turned. "Oh, don't worry about it Roz, we quit."

Her grin was easy as she had two agents of her own flagging her. "There is no quitting. Now, why don't you all be a dear and follow us."

I shook my head. "If you want me to come with you, you're going to have to make me."

She laughed. "Oh, honey, that can be arranged."

"You want to take me on, Roz? See if you're as good as you think you are, or if you trained me to be as good?"

"Lyra, you'll only hurt yourself. You know I just wanted to look after you."

"Bullshit."

I raised my gun and fired. Just close enough for the bullet to whizz by her ear, singeing off a part of her hair.

Her eyes went wide. "How dare you?"

"Don't worry, I'm a believer in preserving human life. Besides, it's my understanding that there are some very important people at Exodus who want to talk to you. So why don't you come with us instead, and we'll see how this plays out."

Her two flanking guards came forward, and she shook her head. "Oh no, she's mine. I think it's time I teach this bitch a lesson."

"Oh, this should be interesting. Because something tells me this was how my mother felt. Wasn't she better than you?"

That was it. The words needed to tip her into crazy town.

She lunged at me. I knew from her training that when you fought angrily, you fought stupidly. And when you fought stupidly, your opponent wins. I was hoping that was going to work to my advantage.

20

LYRA

I could almost feel Marcus's disapproval. "Lyra, we don't have time for this."

On the contrary, I thought we did have time for it. After all, if Roz was occupied with us, her teams would be floundering without their leader, and that was a good thing. Exodus could sweep them all up.

"Lyra, stop this nonsense, and we won't kill your friends."

Addie stepped by my side. "I know how this is supposed to go. You two duke it out mano a mano to see who's best, the student or the teacher. And we're supposed to stand here and watch. But I'm bored."

Her motions were so swift that even I didn't see her intentions until the last second when she shot one of Roz's hulking bodyguards. Headshot. Clean kill. Zero remorse. Marcus already had his gun out and aimed it at bodyguard number two's temple. The two of them were astonishing.

"Mate, you don't want to try me today. You've had my woman for three days, and I'm not inclined to let you live. But on account of wanting to look like a good guy for her, I don't want to shoot you in cold blood. So I'm going to need you to put out your arms all civilized while I cuff you. Or," he jangled his gun, "we take door number one. Your choice really."

Addie turned to me. "Can you get to killing her already? I'm cold and hungry and I want a hot bath and to convince Rhodes I'm hotter than his fiancée, so speed this up, will you?"

I stared at Roz for a long pause. "You had everything. Power, success, but you wanted, what? More? To run with terrorists? Is this how you saw yourself, scurrying like a rat in the sewer?"

"You don't know anything about it. You're sight is so narrow."

"Only you understand. Is that it? Well, It's a good thing you like deep dark holes because you're never going to see the light of day again."

Her brows lifted. "You don't want to see if you can best me?"

I shrugged. "I already have."

Roz's brows lifted. "Hardly, love. You had to be rescued."

"Maybe. But I had *real family* that came for me. This is what it feels like. Not someone controlling me."

"I knew what was best for you."

"You keep saying that. But let's see, you've killed my parents, you tried to kill me, you tried to control my career and every aspect of my life. But in the end, I reject everything about you, you are not my mother and never will be."

Her eyes flared before she snapped and lunged for me. I sidestepped easily, letting my hand slide up the arm she was reaching to punch me with. Then I very deliberately stepped into her space, ensuring my hips would be past hers.

With my leg, I swept hers, and Roz tumbled down. I stood over her, watching. "All this because you couldn't control me. Because I have better influences. You wanted me dead."

"Because you saw the fucking file. If you hadn't seen it, everything would be business as usual."

I didn't help her out. "There is no coming back from a hit squad, Roz. No explanation makes it at all okay." And because I needed to know, I asked, "The car bomb... Did you at least do it yourself?"

She glowered up at me. "It was supposed to be just your mother. He wasn't supposed to be there. She was the intended target."

I waited for the rage as I stared down at her. It didn't come, but that didn't stop me from punching her with a tight, straight jab.

Marcus pulled me back before I could do much more. Addie was there with the zip ties.

I struggled in his hold. "Relax, love. I have you."

And he did. Even as the halls were suddenly flooded with both Exodus and Firm agents, he wrapped his arms around me and kept it all out with his broad shoulders.

"I have you. You're okay."

Meeting his gaze, I smiled. "Now that you're here, I am. I love you."

His smile was easy. "I know. You were just taking your sweet time to say it."

"Were you always this impossible?"

"I was. Now, let's get you home."

"That sounds like a fantastic idea."

21

LYRA

"Oh my God, yes, right there. Right there. Marcus, oh my God."

Marcus was in his favorite spot. Planted right between my legs, torturing me relentlessly with his tongue and his fingers.

As his thumb stroked over my clit, he glanced up with a wicked smile. "Love, you don't think that we survived all this mess for me not to celebrate, do you?"

I laughed. "But somehow this is always your favorite position."

"Ah, yes, you've caught me. It's where I go when I'm happy, when I'm sad, when I just want you to say my name over and over and over again. It's my default."

"Yes, it's your default. Now if you don't mind, could you maybe, just possibly, let me come?"

He laughed. "Nope. Not yet."

And then he carried on for at least another twenty minutes while orgasm after orgasm crashed into me, and I begged, pleaded with him, to let me take a breath. A water break. We'd barely slept all night, and he'd woken me up like he was on a mission.

Part of me was worried he thought that this was going to be our last chance for a while. His team had taken Roz into custody and back to Exodus headquarters. And Lord only knew where and how she was being questioned. That had left The Firm reeling.

Addie and I had gone in for a debriefing. And surprisingly, I'd been released. Browning had just said that he'd be in touch.

And they'd given me an escort. I knew I was being surveilled, sure, but I wasn't under lock and key. Considering everything that had happened, that made perfect sense. But I couldn't help the sense of foreboding that something was going to happen. I was waiting for the other shoe to drop, fearing they were going to separate us.

I think Marcus thought the same thing, because he had been even more attentive than usual.

He'd waited for me outside The Firm. He made it very clear to Browning that if Addie and I didn't come out in a reasonable amount of time, he was coming in. And nobody would like that.

Browning had just looked him up and down, given him a smirk, and escorted me and Addie inside.

We were separated then of course. My best friend had practically strutted. "Shouldn't take long at all, Lyra, I'm ready to tell the truth."

"Right, the truth."

For her, the truth was simple. An agent called in distress. Discovered another agent at the very top was working with terrorists. Simple.

For me, it was more complicated.

Marcus's voice jarred me from my thoughts. "You're not focusing."

Okay, so I might have drifted.

He nipped at my clit with his teeth, and I screamed as another orgasm slapped me in the face, twice. Because as soon as I started to come, he pumped his fingers inside of me, grazing my clit, pushing that little button deep inside my channel. Circling it with the pads of his fingers. I started to shake and tried to clamp my thighs together, but his shoulders were in the way. "Oh no, you don't. I'm not done."

I wasn't sure how much longer it had been when I was laying there, limp, as Marcus finally kissed the inside of my thigh before starting to crawl up my body. He kissed up the center of my chest, ignoring my nipples, which I was honestly grateful for because everything was so sensitive now. He talked into my neck. "Lyra, are you weak, love?"

"Uh-huh." I mumbled incoherently.

And then I could feel him sliding into me, and my eyes flew open. "Oh."

He grinned at that. "That's right. I'm still here." And despite my body feeling limp and loose and the exhaustion that clouded my vision, I wrapped my arms around him and went along for another ride as he started to build another release inside me. One I didn't know if I had in me. One I was almost certain was going to make me pass out.

On my nightstand, my phone rang. "I need to get that."

"Uh-huh. Go ahead."

I stared at him. "Marcus, I—" He rolled his hips just right, making a shiver run through my body.

"I'm not going anywhere, so either you ignore it, or you can answer it and have fun while you're chatting."

"Marcus, I can't talk with you inside me."

"Why not?" he asked with the devil's own grin, leaning in and nipping at my shoulder.

"Because you're distracting me."

"What? Me, distracting? Love, I think you're maligning my character." He was being impossible.

"In a good way. You're distracting in a good way. Oh my god, Marcus, please, please, please?"

Finally, Marcus reached over to my nightstand, grabbed my phone, unplugged it, and handed it to me after he slid the Answer switch on.

And then he grinned evilly as he started to thrust faster.

"Hello?"

Director Browning's voice sounded in my ear. "Agent Wilkinson."

I gasped. "Oh God, sir. Sorry it took me so long to answer."

Marcus, the asshole, kept grinding his hips. Pumping in and out of me. He grabbed one of my ass cheeks and slid his finger between them and started to play with my ass. "Oh, sir, God. Can I call you right back?"

"Agent Wilkinson, this is urgent. We need to speak."

"Oh, right, yes, I'll come right in."

"No, not right now. As requisite after a mission, you need downtime. But I did want to call and tell you that there will be no repercussions for your illicit activities with Agent Black from Exodus."

Marcus just squeezed my ass harder, continuing to pump and thrust.

"No repercussions. Right. That's good news, sir."

"Yes, the intel we had been receiving from Roz was faulty. We discovered she was making it appear as if Exodus had been behind several incidents of terrorist activity. It's bad."

"Yes, sir. I'm sure it is."

"Just know that The Firm values you as an agent. On Monday, we would like to discuss with you how to move forward and what your new responsibilities and duties will be."

Marcus leaned his head down a little as he plumped up one breast with a hand. And then he sucked one nipple into his mouth. Hard.

"Oh my God. New duties, sir?"

Browning was quiet for a moment. "Agent Wilkinson, are you paying attention?"

"Yes, sir, I am. What new duties?"

"After much review through the night, Control would like to make you the temporary branch director."

"In Roz's position?"

"As *acting* director for the time being. You've obviously proven yourself, and you exhibit all of the qualities we'd want in someone who is in charge of other agents. And you've demonstrated that you will do whatever it takes to protect The Firm. So, when you come in again on Monday, we'll talk about the responsibilities and what you'll need to get up to speed."

"But sir, I'm a field agent."

"Oh yes, well, directors do go into the field. It's just not often. That was Roz's personal request. I think she was always concerned about what could happen on a mission."

"Sir, thank you for this opportunity."

"Don't thank me. It's a lot of work, but you've earned it. We'll discuss it more in a few days."

"Yes, sir."

I hung up with him just as Marcus started to grind harder, faster. "Marcus, I, oh my God."

He chuckled. "I want to find out what that call was about, but give me two seconds."

And that was when he went wild. Hands fisting in my hair. Teeth grazing and biting ever so gently into my neck, his pace increased. And then, over and over and over again, he loved me. His hips unrelenting until all I could do was hold on for the ride and call out his name over and over again.

And when I came, he lifted his head so he could watch me. And that was when he finally came with me.

Minutes or maybe even an hour after we'd both come down, he was trailing his fingers up and down my sternum. His voice was low as he asked, "So, they're making you the new Roz?"

"I don't even know what that means."

"Is it something you want?"

"Well, I don't really know. She's always been there. I've never even considered it."

"Well, then it's something to consider now."

"And Browning said that there is evidence to show that Exodus was never working with any terrorist group."

He chuckled. "Didn't I tell you?"

"You know, there's no reason to be smart about it."

"Well, I tried to tell you."

"I know, I know. I just... I can't believe this is how everything turned out."

"Hey, all that matters is that you're safe now."

"Yeah, I know. Thanks to the man I love."

His fingers paused then. Just over my heart. "You know, I never thought I'd hear you say that."

"Yeah, well, it took me a while to realize that I love you." I turned my head toward his.

"And I love you, Lyra Wilkinson."

"So what does this mean?"

"It means that my girlfriend, the woman I love, is a badass agent." He smirked. "Though I'm also a badass agent who saves your life from time to time."

"You know, I've saved your life once or twice, too."

His smile twisted into one of mock disbelief. "Well, if I remember correctly, you tried to kill me."

"If I'd wanted you dead, you'd be dead."

He chuckled. "Yes, I do acknowledge that. You could have easily killed me, but you didn't. So sure, we'll call that saving my life for now."

"Agent Marcus Black, does this mean we're dating?"

"Oh, no, this doesn't mean we're dating. This means that

we're practicing for our future lives together. I've wasted enough time with you. Now that I finally have you on this I-love-you train, I plan to marry you. Someday, not right away. I'm going to let you get used to the idea first."

"Oh, that's awfully generous of you."

"It is, isn't it?" Then he leaned down and brushed my lips softly. "I love you, Agent Lyra Wilkinson. You're my badass, and aren't I the lucky one?"

I laughed at that. "You most certainly are."

THE END

Love spy romance? Make sure to check out my Gentlemen Rogues Series, starting with The King

What's worse than a gorgeous one-night stand who doesn't remember you? Having to pretend to be his wife. For work. The Rogues Division is a top-secret, highly-classified, "I'd tell you but I'd have to kill you" kind of organization. The kind of organization the government pretends not to love having at its disposal.
And we just got our newest recruit…Lachlan King, the sexy billionaire playboy who seduced me into one night of wild, soul-shattering, sex.
When I slipped out of his bed three months ago, I never expected to see him again. My future is set. I'm going to be a Rogues field agent. And field agents don't date. Not to mention it's forbidden to date each other. I'm relieved when he also pretends not to know me, so we can avoid any office awkwardness--until I realize **he isn't pretending**.
Even worse luck, I'm assigned to play his lover in the field. Okay, okay, deep breath. This mission will be easy. All I need to do is pretend to be madly in love with him and make sure neither of us die. Oh and remember this isn't real. I've got to

remember that. I cannot let this playboy seduce me again no matter what my belly does when he looks at me like I'm his. Lachlan "the King," however, has thrown himself into our undercover assignment a little too whole heartedly. He's hell bent and determined on being as convincing as possible. But there's no way I'm letting him fake-husband me back into bed. I won't fall for him this time. I won't. Will I?

ABOUT NANA MALONE

USA Today Best Seller, Nana Malone's love of all things romance and adventure started with a tattered romantic suspense she "borrowed" from her cousin.

It was a sultry summer afternoon in Ghana, and Nana was a precocious thirteen. She's been in love with kick butt heroines ever since. With her overactive imagination, and channeling her inner Buffy, it was only a matter a time before she started creating her own characters.

Now she writes about sexy royals and smokin' hot bodyguards when she's not hiding her tiara from Kidlet, chasing a puppy who refuses to shake without a treat, or begging her husband to listen to her latest hairbrained idea.

ABOUT NANA MALONE

USA Today Best Seller, Nana Malone's love of all things romance and adventure started with a tattered romantic suspense she "borrowed" from her cousin.

It was a sultry summer afternoon in Ghana, and Nana was a precocious thirteen. She's been in love with kick butt heroines ever since. With her overactive imagination, and channeling her inner Buffy, it was only a matter of time before she started crafting her own characters.

Now she writes about sexy royals and smokin' hot bodyguards when she's not hiding her face from Kidlet, chasing a puppy who refuses to skate without a coat, or begging her husband to listen to her latest hairbrained idea.